JOSEPH COVINO JR

ARABIAN NIGHTS LOST: CELESTIAL VERSES I

AN EPIC PRESS BOOK

Published by *Epic Press*
PO Box 30108
Walnut Creek, CA 94598

Library of Congress Control Number:
2002111046

ISBN: 0-943283-06-X

First *Epic Press* Edition published 2005

CONTENTS

JOSEPH COVINO JR

For Evelyn, a true princess of one of the purest and most perfect realms—Christian faith

MESSAGE TO READERS

To those who doubt the realism of *Jamila*, the Jinni and Princess of the Sea, carefully contemplate the following quote:

"We have all known women who sacrificed everything despite themselves, as it were, for the most worthless of men. The world stares and scoffs and blames and understands nothing. There is for every woman one man and one only in whose slavery she is 'ready to sweep the floor.' Fate is mostly opposed to her meeting him but, when she does, adieu husband and children, honor and religion, life and 'soul.'"—Sir Richard F. Burton, Translator of *The Arabian Nights' Entertainments*

PROLOGUE:
MESSENGER OF GOD

THE THUNDER

"It is He who makes the lightning flash upon you, inspiring you with fear and hope, as He gathers up the heavy clouds. The thunder sounds His praises, and the angels, too, for awe of Him. He hurls His thunderbolts at whom He pleases. Yet the unbelievers wrangle about Allah. Stern is His punishment."—Surah XIII, 12-13

JOSEPH COVINO JR

Pandemonium filled the heavens and the earth as the overpowering Hand of Allah, the Almighty and All-Powerful God, lashed the world's waters into a tumultuous and unbridled fury, and swept the great and bounding sea into a seething inferno of a storm.

Flashing bursts of lightning shot their jagged and forked fire-bolts streaking across the deeply darkened skies with blinding brilliance. Booming thunderclaps cracked frightfully through the storm-smitten air. Torrents of rain, falling in solid-looking sheets, showered down heavily out of the thick black rain-clouds churning violently overhead. Turbulent, howling winds whipped and roared furiously across the stormy sea surface, catching dead in the middle of their raging maelstrom a single, solitary ship—helpless, crippled and utterly alone.

Into an uproarious turmoil the deep blue sea convulsed and boiled over. Riotous and rushing waves heaved to mountainous heights—tossing, tumbling, rampaging. Together with the billowing waves and blustering winds the rumbling onslaught of rain ferociously dashed and battered the disabled ship, plying precariously the stampeding seas but then careening desperately out of control.

She was a double-ended galley ship of the smaller dromon runner class—light, long, lean and built for speed, her heavy wooden oars flailing rhythmically in the stormy waters to propel her narrow and curved teakwood hull. Both her stem and stern were sharply pointed and highly raised, looking like the horns of a drowning oxen bubbling up inside of a gigantic cauldron. With the pursuing and unrelenting blast of the storm blowing forcefully at her rear she hurtled dangerously fast over the roving, rough-and-tumble waters. Merging winds and waves slammed into her with gargantuan strength, almost hoisting her across the surface, rocking her hull with moving mountains of water which hit repeatedly like so many gigantic battering rams. As each waved plowed into her, spurting explosively upon impact, she reeled and bobbed, her bow rising and falling wildly upon the crest of each surging swell. Each time her bow plunged downward and banged into a sinking trough, running sheets of seawater sloshed over her sides, swirling and submerging her decks beneath the frothing and foaming waves.

With an ever-growing frenzy the wind blew on, bringing with it the rampant rain and—except for abrupt blazes of lightning—the deepest dark of night. Buffeted and soaked by the wind-flung rain the captain and his men were out on deck in the tumult of the storm, struggling to save their imperiled ship. Mounting water raised the stern high and rammed her bow down with thudding blows into exploding peaks of waves, colliding and spewing with spray over and over again. Over her rails on either side the seas crashed in pounding and thundering surges, engulfing the seamen fighting their way along the decks to climb or grapple with her tarred hemp rigging. She wheeled from the blows and lurched sideways, cleanly snapping many of the stiff and taut ropes seamen had lashed and secured. By fitful and flickering flashes of lightning her grizzled and weatherworn captain looked on in anguish as wind and waves whisked many of his seamen over board, or from their tenuous perches on the ship's quivering shroud and crescent-shaped boom, swept them into oblivion.

"Furl those sails!" the young ship's mate shouted again from the aftermost quarterdeck.

Wide-eyed he watched as the seamen remaining on deck below, clinging tenaciously to their pulley-guided sheets and lines, lowered and lashed the ship's two wildly flapping square-flaxen mainmast and foremast sails. Struggling to keep his foothold he left the steersman holding the port steering oar and stumbled across the slippery deck to lay hold of the overtaxed tiller—greatly strained by the wrenching tug of the sea. Along with his captain and helmsman the arms of all three grimacing seamen intertwined, straining every nerve to keep their flimsy grip upon the slick tiller-post. Into each other's reddened, rain-spattered faces they yelled loudly to be heard before their voices faded into the din of the storm.

Looking extremely long-faced the mate reported their calamitous state.

"All the sails are lashed, Captain, but the storm is still driving us from dead astern!"

"Come about and steer into the wind!" the captain commanded.

"Impossible, Captain!" the helmsman shook his head with a frightened urgency. "The rudder has no hold against the water! She's running before the wind on bare poles!"

"Hold our course then! If this wind hits us broadside we'll capsize!"

"We can't, Captain!" the mate blurted out in desperate dissent. "We've thrown out all our anchors already! We're barely keeping an even keel!"

"You've cast all anchors astern?"

"Aye, Captain! And the grappling hooks! It's hopeless! She's at the mercy of the wind!"

Abruptly the captain's face turned hopelessly grave with despair as he prayed.

"May Allah preserve us."

Deep in the bowel of the ship below hardworking galley slaves laboriously pulled their long pine oars to a dinning drumbeat. A plaited leather whip lashed out at their sweaty, sinewy backs. Snapping the whip was a burly and bald slave-driver hovering over them—oppressively—as he stomped across the long gangway, running the level length of the rectangular deck of the inner hull and cutting a centered aisle through the bank of grimy, herring bone-arranged thwarts—their acute angles pointed toward the stern. Repulsing and sickening the senses was the filthy, suffocating stench of fifty half-naked, toiling men confined and crowded into the cramped slave-deck.

"Row, you accursed dogs!" the slave-driver barked. "Row—before I flay the flesh from your bones with a thousand stripes!"

JOSEPH COVINO JR

His whip cracked menacingly.

"Row, I say! Harder! Put your backs into it or you'll have no backs!"

Again and again his whip cracked—mercilessly, relentlessly—prompting one among the younger and stronger galley slaves to turn, look up and glare defiantly—his deep-set eyes showing a piercing hostility. When the whip next lashed out it bit into one of the young slave's well-muscled bare arms, streaking it with a stinging bloody band.

"What do you gawk at, slave?" the slave-driver growled. "Keep your Roman dog's face forward or I'll flog your eyes out!"

Looking sullen the young slave submitted silently and rowed on.

On the deck above the captain cupped his hands around his mouth and shouted up to the lookout perched precariously high in the ship's swaying crow's nest—high atop the masthead amidships.

"Keep a sharp lookout aloft there and tell us what you see!"

"Aye, Captain!" the lookout shouted back. "Something looms far off in the middle of the sea—glowing now black and then bright—and we're on a collision course!"

"We've lost our course and gone far astray—with no hope of return," the captain muttered to himself.

As the captain's face abruptly blanched and turned blank with fear his mate looked aghast. Afraid, he stared at his captain with pleading eyes.

"Is there no turning her back, Captain?"

"No," the captain sounded undeniably certain. "We cannot stay this vessel! The wind has gotten mastery over us and driven us to the outermost seas of the world. Unless God grants us a means of escape we're all dead men."

"Where is the storm heading us?"

"To the Sea of Peril and the Magnet Mountain—upon which no man ever fell and came away alive. Whoever goes there will surely die—with no hope of escape."

"Magnet Mountain?"

"A towering stone of ebony gifted by God with a strange and mysterious attraction for iron—toward which the currents will carry us whether we will it or not—and which no ship can approach in safety, for it will split our sides wide open and every last nail in plank will fly out and stick fast to it. Since the days of old no one but the Most High knows how many vessels have been smashed upon its rocks."

"Then we are dead men," his mate sounded forlorn and resigned.

In despair the captain's voice confirmed their worst fate and fear.

"None of us can be saved."

Back below deck the slave-driver bent his whip in the tight grip of his beefy fist and bent down by the young Roman galley slave upon whose arm he had carved a belt of blood. Snarling, he abruptly poked the doubled-over end of his whip into the young slave's cheek—hard, nudging his head aside.

"I've never liked you much, oarsman," he sneered, "because you smell like the son of a dog."

Grimacing from pain the young slave recoiled from the whip and calmly lifted up his eyes to his brawny intimidator.

"It's been said that the voice of an ass is the loudest and most ugly of voices," he said sedately.

"You insolent dog!" the slave-driver's jowly face abruptly flushed with rage as he quickly drew back his whip-hand.

Instinctively—his oar chains and manacles clanking—the young slave ducked and dug his bearded chin deep into his chest, tucking his head beneath his shoulders to evade the slave-driver's back-handed blow and the pitiless scourging which succeeded. That was when the massive timber beam crashed down from the ceiling, sprawling the slave-driver flat onto the gangplank and pinning him beneath its ponderous weight. Growling like a trapped animal he struggled violently to wriggle free as the galley slave, seeing his startling predicament, groped and grabbed frantically to yank from his waist-cord the keys to the galley oar-locks. Fumbling in his excitement the galley slave hurried to turn a key in the iron padlocks to unchain the manacles shackling his wrists and ankles to the oars and rowing bench. After freeing himself he immediately turned and reached out to the haggard rower next to him, sitting chained to the same slanted rowing bench they shared as a pair. Quickly he turned the key in the padlock enchaining him, only the other rower resisted and grappled with the young slave's fumbling fingers, breaking off the key inside the lock!

"What are you doing, man, are you mad? I'm trying to free you!"

"You can free no one!" the resistant rower said. "This ship and all aboard her are doomed! All you can do is save yourself, for only you will survive her."

"What are you raving about?"

"Hear me and obey, for I am a messenger of God who comes from the Sixth Heaven."

Slowly but surely the messenger's hands were hardening and turning into a lustrous, sapphire-green—slowly crystallizing his entire body, creeping along from the outer extremities of his limbs and rapidly spreading to his torso.

"Your hands!" the young slave cried. "What's happening to you?"

"The kingdom from which I come was formed of the green sapphire—as I too was formed—so my time in this world is almost at an end."

"Only a madman would claim to have come sent by God!"

"There is sure pleasure in being mad which none but madmen know. But there is also safety in knowing that which I alone can tell you—which only a messenger of God can tell you!"

"Speak plainly then!" the young slave yelled rashly. "This is no time for idle talk!"

"Allah is enough of a witness between you and me—and

whoever has knowledge of The Book," the messenger shouted, "so listen carefully to me and heed my words: in such a place near to you is a devout woman. You must go to her and be at her command!"

"There is no Majesty and there is no Might except God! What place? What woman?"

"On the Isle of Pearl in the Temple of Worship atop the Mountain of the Clouds—a devotee named Fatima! Go to her and be at her command! But beware! And again I say: beware of the Sentinels—the Stallions of the Seashore, for if they overtake you they will surely destroy you! So beware, although there is no flight from fate and lot!"

"Caution avails me nothing against fate and lot!"

"Caution avails me nothing against time—which now makes me tremble—for time is powerful and severe. I used to row without being weary, but now I am too weary to row and my time is run out! God be with you!"

Soon the messenger's entire body turned into one glassy, spindle-shaped figure which cracked and splintered into countless, shiny crystalline and prismatic-looking gemstones then littering the place where he sat as a rower. For a moment the young slave looked sadly at the empty spot.

"And with you."

In the rapidly approaching distance the captain and his storm-beleaguered crew could then see clearly the craggy and lofty magnetic monolith soaring into the turbulent thunderheads above, flashing and radiating its beamy, luminescent light—lapis lazuli in color—through the tempest and across the deep blue waters. Solemnly the captain looked into the faces of his officers.

"There is no Majesty and there is no Might except in God, the Glorious, the Great! Man cannot prevent that which is foreordained of Fate! By God we have fallen upon a place of sure destruction and there is no way of escape for any of us—and none of us can be saved!"

Then he leaned out over the quarterdeck's railing and shouted out to his valiant but doomed crew an emotional farewell.

"Hear me, my brothers, and God preserve you! Pray, all of you, to the Most High, that He deliver us from this strait! Beg your deliverance of Him and lament yourselves, for if among you is no righteous man whose prayers the Lord will accept, we are taking our leave of one another!"

Up onto the gangplank the young galley slave scrambled, stumbling for footing on the flooding and sloping deck overflowing with the cold, invading waters. Suddenly he felt a wrenching hand clamp around one of his ankles, forcing him to fall headlong onto the gangplank. From beneath the heavy timber beam the hulking slave-driver was squirming his way free and had a vise-like grip on one of the young slave's legs. Twisting his tightly clenched leg the slave quickly recoiled and rolled onto his back, kicking his free foot savagely into the slave-driver's fattened face—repeatedly until the grip on his other leg relaxed and let go.

He regained his footing when the slave-driver freed himself completely and clambered awkwardly from beneath the timber beam, his body bloodied but briskly moving. Footing on the running gangplank was slippery and difficult to keep since the ship leaned even more obliquely than before—water gushing in from the hatchway opening up to the deck above for which the slave was heading. Again the slave-driver groped for him, laying firm hold of his waist. Stumbling the slave fell but clasped both of his hands together, slamming them down hard in one big fist against the slave-driver's head, making him reel from the blow momentarily. He slipped when he felt the slave-driver's clutching hold on him relax again, but scrambled faster up the ladder to the hatchway above, supporting himself on one leg while wildly kicking with the other to beat back the slave-driver still grasping in pursuit.

Then the whole ship rocked under the impact of the raging rollers pounding and thundering directly over her, making her pitch and roll wrenchingly. Flooding black water overspread the floor after seeping in from tarred cracks in the splitting seams, mingling into a single sheet which eddied and whirled all around the rowers' legs and feet. As far as the rafters reached little else but water abruptly overran the entire lower deck, which soon turned into a chaotic upheaval of tumbling wood and bodies.

Then the whole hull shook convulsively. Timber beams grated and rattled. Dirt flaked down from the ceiling cross-pieces. Flickering lamps swayed wildly. Water gushed in from her arched oar ports. Deadly flying objects filled the air: iron nails and planking pegs whizzed across the room. Unseen, unheard, impossible to dodge—they struck, killed or kept flying until they impaled flesh or wood. Then the deck swam deep in stinging, swirling, bitter-tasting saltwater.

Jolted, jarred and awash with water the whole deck began to break up. One after another the ceiling's massive timber beams banged down into the jumbled turmoil below. Onto the deck the upper deck crumbled and spilled. Walls caved in, fracturing into broken planks which fell whirling in the wash of the wreckage. Finally the hull itself buckled and collapsed with water crashing in behind it, foaming and frothing crimson with blood—a babble of shrieks and screams from thrashing and trapped men mixing in with the confused din of destruction.

Bit by bit the ship's hull pulled apart. Her decks crumpled up and began breaking in half. Seams ruptured and split open everywhere. Ribs spread and burst wide apart. Hollow oar blades broke off, falling to pieces. Her long, stern-hung rudder cracked in two and shattered. Her mast cracked and toppled over. Soon the whole ship collapsed into one great mass of floating firewood.

Once out on the tilting upper deck the young slave leapt from the ship to freedom, jumped into the surging seas and clambered up onto a wide, floating piece of heavy planking. Out of nowhere the pursuing slave-driver leapt onto the planking after him, nearly sinking them both. Only this time his pursuer clenched in his fist a grappling iron and fell on top of him too quickly for his prey to escape. As the slave rolled over onto his back, rising to fight off his attacker in a death struggle, the slave-driver clenched his throat, ramming him back down hard against the unyielding wood and raising his arm to strike with the grapnel—the sharp sight of which struck terror into the slave's eyes.

"Dog! I'll send you to the briny bottom!" the slave-driver bellowed.

Just as sudden and unexpected some sort of strange, slate-colored and spindle-shaped creature sprang at one jump from the sea—lithe, smooth-skinned and hairless—leaping into the stormy air and onto the strapping slave-driver's back, shrieking a high-pitched squeal and showing a glimpse of a prominent forehead, small flashing, copper-colored eyes, gleaming chisel-shaped teeth and a low, ridge-like fin rising midway down the spine as the creature latched onto his body and held tenaciously fast. Unable to trust his senses all the slave could do was look agape as the thing from the sea—whatever it was—clung tightly to the slave-driver, wrapping human-looking but flipper-like and willowy limbs around his flailing body and plunging back with him into the ocean, disappearing from sight beneath the billowing waves. Before long the waves washed the young slave off his planking and into the heavy, ever-roughening seas; and for all he knew he too was a drowned, dead man.

Only he was neither drowned nor dead. Somehow, sometime later on he landed ashore upon some strange, unknown and unfamiliar seacoast, awash with the roaring, rolling surf crashing at its edge. With the stormy wind and rain whipping all about him he staggered out of the water and toppled over headlong, collapsing heavily from exhaustion onto the soft white beach which spilled over with the onrushing tidewater, running and retreating over its soggy, sandy banks.

Nor was he alone. Once he crawled up sluggishly onto higher and drier ground, dragging himself weakly across the sand

and rolling over onto his back, flagging from fatigue, a tall and undulating shadow cast by some unseen presence approached and crossed his supine body. Just as he blacked out, lapsing into deep unconsciousness, the thing bending over him reached out with one dark gray, fluke-tipped limb. Gently it touched and turned his wet and weary face, but his eyes were already heavily closed.

CHAPTER ONE: DEVOTEE OF THE HEAVENS

THE MOUNTAIN

"By the Mountain, and by the Scripture penned on unrolled parchment; by the Visited House, the Lofty Vault, and the swelling sea, your Lord's punishment shall surely come to pass! No power shall ward it off."—Surah, LII, 1-8

JOSEPH COVINO JR

L ying prone upon the sand with his face resting upon his hands the young galley slave awoke—still spent from his ordeal but feeling rested and relaxed. A soothing warm sea breeze blew gently over him. Wincing from the bright sunlight he blinked open his eyes and lingered, listening contentedly to the breakers rolling in and falling onto the seashore. Upon his lips he still tasted salt. Almost instantly his nostrils flared: he smelled the aroma of food—succulently cooked food. He heaved himself up on his arm and found spread wondrously beside him a savory looking meal.

Set out before him was a large round-tinned copper tray of food, supported by a small stand and warmed by a small earthenware pot, half-buried in the sand and aglow with live hot coals. In the tray small chopped pieces of butter-cooked lamb stewed in vegetables together with some butter-boiled seasoned rice. Round the rim of the tray he ran a finger and found it inlaid with tortoise-shell. Spread upon the ground next to the tray was a round embroidered cloth upon which rested a porous earthen bottle of fresh water. He marveled at the unexpected sight, looking around and about for whoever could have plausibly laid the modest table. Then he noticed the footprints—human footprints—impressed in the sand.

Tracks of footprints—conspicuously a single set—betrayed a lot of erratic activity all about the spot at which he rested. But a more constant track of those very same footprints showed a definite, steady and undeviating path treading its way straight to the sea, terminating there at the water's edge. Standing up to brush sand from his body and face the galley slave followed the footpath and strode to the seashore, peering up and down the endless and empty rock-bound coast. A seething sun blazed high up in the clear, cloudless, bright blue sky and beat down oppressively upon the spare strip of white beach. Shielding his eyes from its blinding glare the galley slave pensively watched the ocean toss its gently tumbling waves onto the shore, overspreading and soaking the glistening wet sand. He turned about and stood in awe of the sheer gray limestone cliffs rising abruptly from the sand, soaring a thousand feet or more and forming a continuous seawall, ranging unbroken along the entire length of the distant seacoast. Even more magnificent in the light of day was the remote Magnet Mountain—its deepest ebony coloration shining radiantly—its precipitous peaks towering splendidly but serenely out of the calm ocean offshore.

Kneeling in the surf the galley slave sat upon his haunches to wash and pray. He reached down and took up some seawater cupped in his hands, splashing and rubbing his face, rinsing out his mouth and massaging his beard, ears and neck. Then he wet and wrung his hands, rubbing both arms as high as his elbow at least three times—the right hand and arm first in preparation for eating.

"Ah!" he sighed, arising from the sea. "God is most Great!"

Then he returned to the food-tray and sat down with his right knee raised, following the example of the Prophet—Mohammed—who adopted the custom to avoid too comfortable a sitting-posture while eating—tempting needless and self-indulgent gratification.

"In the Name of God, the Compassionate, the Merciful!" he prayed.

Using the thumb and two fingers of his right hand he drew the first piece of lamb to the edge of the tray and ate it—as he did with the rest of the pieces. After eating he guzzled a long drink of water from the bottle, draining it with an even longer sigh of satisfaction.

"Praise be to God, the Lord of all creatures!"

So busily absorbed with heartily devouring his mysteriously provided meal the galley slave paid no attention to the stout shadow cast over him by the hulking figure lumbering up from behind.

"Did you really think you would escape me, dog?" the startlingly familiar voice growled.

At hearing the sinister, gutturally uttered words the galley slave spun around and rolled to his feet, squatting. Incredibly the brutal and sadistic slave-driver from the galley ship appeared out of nowhere and hovered over him—still brandishing his grappling iron. His fearsome sight took the galley slave unawares and struck him momentarily dumb.

"You!" he gasped.

"Surprised to see me, my old galley dog, and ready to meet your maker?"

"Surprised and sorry, for chancing upon an ass is always said to be a bad omen."

"You will be sorry," the slave-driver snarled, "for I will cure you of your insolent tongue once and for all by plucking it out with this!" He thrust forward the grapnel gripped tightly in his fist, baring the whites of his knuckles. "And by it I will avenge my shipmates whom you cursed to damnation from the day you were clapped in irons."

Just then the two were distracted by a distant but distinct sound—at once arresting and strangely familiar. Intently they listened—silent and still—as the sound drew near and filled the air, growing clearer, more definite and before long unmistakable: horses hooves! Powerful, thundering and rampaging across the strand—the beating hooves shook the very ground they stood upon!

Then they saw them materializing from behind the big rocks bounding the seacoast: brilliantly white Arabian horses—stallions all—galloping herds of them, stampeding along the full length and breadth of the seashore, crowding, thronging and treading before them an explosive path of spurting sand and water. Majestic, spirited and robust, their large heads, arched necks and deep chests carried high and proud, their fiery eyes flashing with fervor and zeal, their long, fine and lustrous manes and erect tails flowing and waving briskly in the wind, their sleek and supple bodies in fast and furious motion—the Arabians blazed a trail perfect in grace and speed. It would yet prove perfect in danger and death.

Straight towards the pair—soundly engrossed by the on-rushing horde—the horses charged! Once more the galley slave heard the godly messenger's voice echoing in his mind through the din of the sea storm: "But beware! And again I say: Beware of the Sentinels—the Stallions of the Seashore, for if they over-take you they will surely destroy you!"

Furtively the galley slave fingered the handle of the fire-pot, slowly but carefully curling his fingers until he had a firm hold on it, judging all the while the nearness of the slave-driver. Abruptly he leapt up and lunged forward, flinging the firepot into the slave-driver's face, sending the red-hot coals flying all over his exposed body. Hurling himself forward the galley slave heaved his knee into the slave-driver's groin and fled for his life. Doubled over the slave-driver sank to his knees, groaning in pain and fumbling frantically to cast off the fiery coals searing his bare skin. His grapnel dropped uselessly to the sand. He stumbled to his feet and hobbled over to the water's edge, plung-ing into the surging surf to salve his severely singed skin.

By then the galley slave bolted to the sea cliff and bounded up onto some low-lying rocks bordering its base, swinging up to a low-level ledge by clinging to a sturdy tree branch protruding from the cliff face. Looking back to the beach he watched in a panting fright as the fleet-footed stallions overtook the stalwart slave-driver, crushing and squashing him between their sweaty and hard-pounding bodies; snapping and champing at him with their gnashing and gnawing teeth; ripping and tearing his flac-cid flesh to shreds and tatters; trampling him to death beneath their heavily stomping hooves until his mercilessly pummeled body slumped, slipped and disappeared into the churning spume—awash with swirling blood. In force the horses chased the galley slave to the foot of the cliff, whinnying in their rav-ening frenzy, their eyes blazing, their nostrils flaring, rearing up on their hind legs and stamping at the cliff face, chipping out splintery rocks with their clopping hooves. Before long they were gone as swiftly as they came, stampeding thunderously along the distant stretch of beach until lost from sight.

Again all was quiet except for the gentle wash of waves, spilling onto the seashore and sloshing about the dead slave-driver's mangled and mutilated body. To his great surprise the galley slave glanced around and found that the ledge he stood upon abutted a narrow and rugged footpath, which turned and twisted its way up the sheer, craggy cliff face, rising steeply in tortuous and terraced steps to the top of the precipice. Unscathed but afraid to descend to the seashore he climbed and picked his way up the escarpment, carefully scaling the roughhewn, serrated steps. His feet slipped upon loose rocks which, grating beneath his weight, tumbled together with fractured earth over the crumbly ledge. Gusty winds whipped up and down his feathery-feeling body, threatening to whisk him into limitless space. Out of one danger and into another—he shuddered at the dizzying sight as the ground fell farther and farther away from his flimsy footing.

Like a bolt from the blue the galley slave heard and felt at one fell swoop a shrill graaking cry, a jingle of tiny metal bells together with a sharp, stinging pain pricking the nape of his neck. Impulsively he cringed, groping his neck and lifting up his eyes—looking fearfully skyward. Then he spotted the bold and robust bird—a white falcon—who nosedived from the heavens to strike at him with clawing talons and soared into the sky to attack again. In a steep and swift ascent the falcon shot up, circled, hovered fleetingly and flew—in a spectacular spiral—to a high pitch of speed before stooping to dive again. Frantically the galley slave broke off from the cliff face a jutting tree branch which he tore forcefully from some tenacious creepers. Once more he heard the menacing graaking cry but saw only flashing glimpses of the bird's trim white body, yellow feet, pale beak and dark brown eyes as the falcon swooped down from the sky at top speed—diving in a single, straight, free-falling and relentless attack. With his branch the galley slave swung and swiped at the bird, missing and nearly plunging himself over the ledge.

Suddenly a shrill whistle, twittering loudly, summoned the falcon and the gliding bird rapidly disappeared past the cliff's summit. Touching the nape of his neck the galley slave fingered the blood on his hand. Once he winced and looked skyward again he saw no sky! All was utter darkness as if a colossal cloud had abruptly blacked out the sun! Another deafening cry rang in his ears as stormy gusts of wind blustered all about him, blowing up dust into his face, making him bury his head in his arms. At another fell swoop he felt his stomach sink and saw the rock-bound coast below shrink to puny proportions as the earth fell rapidly and precipitously away from him. A gigantic and monstrous bird, forcefully flapping wings stretching some twenty paces long, snatched him from the cliff's ledge with enormous, scaly talons and lifted his helpless body aloft. Panic-stricken he watched the fissured cliff face plummet past him as he was hoisted higher and higher until the crest of the cliff abruptly cropped up and the bird's mighty talons released their iron grip about his torso—letting him drop and fall into unlimited space—or so he feared.

Tumbling only a short span to the ground the galley slave easily alighted, sprawled, atop a pliant padding of rich, brown, grass-covered earth, scattered in places with broken chunks of black volcanic rock. He got up and stood aghast as the mammoth bird hovered high over the sheer, rock-faced cliff towering above the lofty terrace he had landed upon. From the cliff face jutted jagged peaks and tall trees overgrown with creeping vines. Embedded in the exposed stony surface were the distinctly curved contours of a colossal, pearly Nautilus seashell—into the cavernous mouth of which the monstrous bird flew as if returning to a giant, lofty nest.

Struck with wonder—as one dropped from the clouds—the galley slave arose to survey his newest surroundings. Nearby stood a large rectangular structure, part roofed, part open-air. Open was its transverse forecourt, wider than it was long, fringed by fine-grained colonnades and approached by a short flight of polished stone steps. Roofed was a rectangular bay with a hypo-style hall within, longer than it was wide, adjoining rows of colored marble columns lining its walls and buttressing its ceiling. Inside the hall aisles of columns reached deep from the entry portal—a pointed, keel-shaped, rectangular-edged arch—to the far wall, where a wider central aisle crossed length-wise a transverse aisle, stretching from side to side and fashioning the floor into a T-shaped nave. Its façade was formed of baked terra-cotta—its ceramic tiles cut into small mosaic shapes and fitted into colorful and complex Arabesque designs, framing wall niches and overlaying the arched entry. Embroidered prayer rugs overspread the prayer hall floor. One hemispherical vault of clustered niches—looking like the cells of an ornate and mushrooming honeycomb—hovered over the entry just as another domed over the prayer niche across the chamber.

It was a modest yet magnificent mosque!

Seeing or hearing no living thing the galley slave prudently approached the structure and stepped up into the forecourt. All was quiet except for the soothing sound of trickling water. Inside the arcade-enclosed courtyard stretched a large reflecting pool of still water—adorned and trimmed with a fine, geometrically-patterned pavement of colored marbles, and divided into quarters with a big water basin and fountain set in the middle. Remarkably different about this particular fountain-pool were the fine, chestnut-colored stone statues of five Arabian horses standing each their life-sized heights of some fifteen hands tall at the pool's edge—their delicate and slender, dish-faced heads all looking off in the very same direction but facing away from the pool.

Pensively the galley slave paused to gently stroke with a caressing hand one of the lifeless horse's large and roundly-chiseled cheekbones. Then he prudently passed on, stepping inside and crossing the hushed and shadowed hall, treading softly across the padded floor and passing quietly through the diagonal rows of continuously and perfectly aligned columns. Alert but anxious he strode straight to the incurved, oval prayer-niche, carved and cradled in the middle of the wide stucco wall facing Mecca, covered by a small canopy-dome and lighted by a glass lamp suspended from its apex. A pointed keel-arch having cusped inner edges framed the niche, flanked by twin candelabra with plasterwork emblazoned with glazed ceramic tiles. Running water flowed from a colossal and cavernous clamshell embedded in the middle of the niche and poured into a basin quietly capturing it as it spilled softly over the shell's lower edge. Pausing the galley slave reached out to let water stream gently through his fingers. Reverently he admired and touched with his wet fingertips the continuous Arabesque lines and stems—endlessly entwining, branching, radiating, splitting and interlacing in infinite but constant confusion.

"God is boundless," the human voice abruptly accosting him was at once unmistakably feminine and curiously entrancing, "is He not?"

"Yes He is," the galley slave answered absent-mindedly, hardly realizing he was addressing someone alive and at hand, wheeling around with a quietly choked gasp.

Emerging gradually from shadows spread by pillars was a tall, slender and stately woman of dark and imposing aspect. Wrapped about her to ankle-length was a deep indigo-blue Arabian cloak, hitched at her waist with a belt and embroidered at its edges—along her shoulder line and around her wrists—with gold metal thread. Upon her feet she wore indigo-dyed canvas slippers. A simple black-cotton gauze veil draped her head. Hung about her neck was a long strand of ninety-nine lustrous black-coral prayer beads from the Red Sea, tracing the ninety-nine attributes of God. Inlaid with silver those were sectioned in three clusters of thirty-three beads by two spacer beads and one terminal bead ending with a black tassel. Upon her upraised and slightly outstretched arms, sheathed in a gauntleted glove of heavy leather, was perched her combative white falcon—his head covered with a dry-tanned leather hood; his wings fluttering with mild trepidation.

"Come," she quietly commanded him.

Obediently and silently he followed her through a gallery of arched columns until they emerged outside from an arched portal, setting foot upon a spacious, open-air, balustraded veranda overlooking the vast ocean spreading boundlessly before them over a thousand feet below. Supported by that expansive, sea-viewing veranda was a towering, spiral minaret laid in upright brick grilles, twirling and winding its way up into the clouds. She conveyed her falcon to a tapered block perch, standing erect like an inverted cone driven into the floor, onto which the bird readily alighted. She took off the falcon's hood and the bird vigorously shook himself—his feathers slowly rising and settling as he regained his unruffled composure.

"What has brought you to this place where no man has ever yet come to me?" she asked sedately without turning about.

"Forgive my intrusion, my aunt," the galley slave apologized. "I meant no trespass."

Once the falcon firmly perched himself, poised and at ease, he displayed the very same regal bearing as his keeper, assuming a calm, dignified and proud pose, looking supremely stoical, self-possessed and noble. Leisurely she stood aside to marvel at her falcon's trim and tight-plumaged torso—snowy white with blue-black markings—his hooked, pale-horned beak; his piercing dark brown eyes; and his strong, curved talons holding fast to his tall wooden perch.

"Behold the swiftest and most spectacular of all birds of prey: the fabled white falcon!" she boasted. Abruptly she turned about and let fall the rectangular black cotton headscarf masking her prim lips. "Who are you and how came you to be on this mountain upon which no one has ever fallen?"

"I'm a seafarer, my aunt. I fell into a calamity at sea and was shipwrecked. But by the grace of God—the Almighty and All-Merciful!—I landed safely upon your shores, although perhaps not so safely upon your mountain."

"Even so, the great Roc is the monarch of all the gigantic birds and thrives here. Such a kingly creature—like a king of the realm—can be either a protector or a destroyer—or for you a chariot of the skies."

"Begging my aunt's pardon, but I think I would have preferred my chariot to have stayed upon good solid ground."

"You are unharmed?" She looked suddenly concerned.

"Most parts feel…" The galley slave smiled slightly, lightly rubbing his backside, "uninjured."

"Praise be to God for your safety and protection!" She looked relieved. "No doubt you are an outsider here. What is your name?"

"My name is Yusuf." Respectfully he stepped up to salute her, bowing and kissing softly her extended hand. "Yes, I do admit to being a stranger to this land of which I know nothing. But—by God—I came here not by choice or even of my own free will. Nor was this place the object of my desire, for only a storm at sea compelled me to become stranded upon your shores."

"What then is the object of your desire?"

"Only to wait and look out for some passing ship to take me off. Beyond that I crave only your prayers so perhaps Allah—to Whom belongs all honor and glory!—will through your favor deliver me from my plight."

"Only he who believes that falcons will live forever comes here to this mountain top. You will find for yourself that man cannot escape what is written."

"All I crave to escape is an early death." He smirked slightly. "But I believe the falcons nesting upon your mountain crave to render certain that no visitors live forever."

"The many birds of this mountain serve only to protect and make safe what is written."

"And the horses of your seashore? Do they too protect and make safe what is written?"

"Even so," she nodded sedately, collecting her thoughts.

"Tradition has told how the great King Suleyman commanded one of the Jinn to lead an Arabian stallion of unequaled excellence into the sea—and then bar his return to the shore. Seven colts emerged from the frothing foam where the stallion had sunk into the waves. And each colt sired a noble lineage of the Arabian horse. It is that lineage—and its exalted offspring—which now stands perpetual guard over our shore."

"And what of you, my aunt? Are you perhaps a fortune-teller who divines what is written?"

"If a diviner foretells the fortunes of others it is only because some of the evil Jinn have overheard the talk of angels in the lowest heaven. They have stolen away some of the secret decrees of fate and destiny, and they have carried these back to the diviner's ear. Only the evil Jinn do not speak to me."

"Then you are not of the Jinn?"

"No. Like you I too am a child of mankind."

"Then who are you? And what is this sublime place where only one of the Jinn would live at the very edge of the sea—and so cut off from the rest of the world?"

"My whole life here is devoted to prayer and praising God. Know that I am Fatima—the Devotee—and sole caretaker of this holy shrine and keeper of the sacred scriptures: the Celestial Verses—which you must learn and which I will teach you."

"You bear the name of the daughter of the Prophet."

"As you bear the name of the great liberator of God's disciples."

"Of what would I learn from your teaching, my aunt?"

"Something of your own fate and destiny—that which is written on your own head in the very sutures of your skull—just as it is written at the very beginning of creation on the Preserved Tablet in heaven."

"You are—like the Prophet—a seer of destiny?"

"No one can see truly the appointed destiny of men but God—the Most High—for He decrees all things. But I do see before me a man who is about to find and know his own destiny.

33

Shall we search and find it together?"

"I doubt my desire to know my destiny, my aunt, for fear my fate and fortune approach and its revelations prove to be undesirable."

"Then before we look forward to see what lies ahead we should first look back and consider what has already passed and gone by."

"I don't understand."

"Fear not," she reassured him. "In time—and with God's blessing—you shall understand all and everything. Now tell me your story from first to last—from where do you come and how came you here—and hide of it nothing."

"Hearing is consenting, my aunt. I come from the land of Italy and was born in Rome. And my path to here—as is my story—was a long and extraordinary one."

"How did you come to be so far from your fatherland?"

"Some years ago I lived on the island of Sicily—thought then to be a safe haven from the many Arab attacks which plagued Italy from the south—and which long ago threatened even Rome herself. Most towns on the island paid tribute to Arab pirates to buy their protection. But Syracuse—the town where I lived—had not been raided by Arabs for more than sixty years—an entire generation. But then came a surprise attack by marauding Arabs from Syria—the Saracen despoilers—who only seldom raided the island. I was seized as a white slave and taken by ship to the slave market at Aleppo. There I was traded and sold into a wealthy household in the Round City of Baghdad—the Abode of Peace. Early on I found favor with my master, who trained me for the military guard. He pressed me to embrace Islam since Muslim slaves fared far better in life than Christian ones. A sudden illness took my master's life—and much to my good fortune—he had willed that I be set free upon his death. So I was given my freedom. Only then my good fortune took a terrible turn for the worse and the most extraordinary events came to pass."

TWO:
SEDUCTRESS
OF BAGHDAD

WOMEN

"Men have authority over women because Allah has made them the one superior to the other, and because they spend their wealth to maintain them. Good women are obedient. They guard their unseen parts because Allah has guarded them. As for those from whom you fear disobedience, admonish them and send them to beds apart and beat them. Then if they obey you, take no further action against them. Allah is high, supreme."—Surah, IV, 34

JOSEPH COVINO JR

"I leaned toward licentious living—lewd and lecherous behavior," Yusuf recalled, carrying his thoughts back to a different time and place long since past. "I drifted from the path of rightness, drinking wine by the cupfuls and cavorting with wicked women for days and nights on end. Evil was my condition and troubled was my mind. Spring had arrived—with its roses and trees in full bloom—and the city's waters were overflowing. And it was feverishly hot."

§

The market Bazaar in the Imperial Capital and Round City of Baghdad , the Abode of Peace, in the year 806 A.D.

Yusuf paused to refresh himself at the ornate street fountain overhung by a red-shingled dome beneath which an unlit lantern was suspended at its apex. Water poured freely from a spigot protruding from an arched wall-niche emblazoned with lustrous glazed ceramics. Leaning upon the beautified basin he reached out to catch some running water with cupped hands, splashing and rubbing it all over his heat-flushed face.

Sweltering air and dust wafted together in rising, stifling swells as the hot sun beat down oppressively upon the crowded city streets, swarming with the bustling and endlessly moving horde of noisy people, animals and goods. Yusuf leisurely strolled into the shade of the large, covered market-pavilion, where slanting rays of dusty sunlight filtered down through the open hatchways in the arched canopy hung high overhead. From their narrow rows of shops—small booths and stalls—lining each side of the extensive market thoroughfare, spirited merchants eagerly traded their salable wares: rice, wheat and linens from Egypt; fruits from Syria; spices from the East Indies; glassware from Lebanon; gold from Nubia; ivory from Africa; rubies and dyes from India; carpets and fabrics from Armenia; rugs and perfumes from Persia; silks and brocades from Arabia—and far more sights, sounds and scents than human senses could ever possibly perceive or appreciate.

Yusuf shouldered his way through the teeming crowd. A rider sitting astride an ambling donkey jostled him. A crier shouting bids for auctioned goods made him flinch. He shook his head and waved away with a dismissive expression a peddler hawking animal hooves. He passed through the food market, stopping at a butcher's stall, and found a stout, red-faced, turbaned shopkeeper slumbering peacefully upon his upraised bench, snugly clasping his pudgy hands over his rounded belly. Saying nothing Yusuf took from a table-set earthen platter a morsel of mutton wrapped in a banana leaf and raised it to his parted lips to bite. His eyes still shut the quietly snoozing shopkeeper suddenly assumed an attitude of joviality and calmly held out his open, upturned palm. Smiling, Yusuf reached into his cotton waist belt pocket, dropped a coin into the shopkeeper's outstretched hand and passed on.

Yusuf came to a dealer in knives and stopped to intently inspect the stall's large display rack of glinting dagger blades—hung edge to edge and overlapping like a bird's plumage.

"May God help?" asked the attending vendor.

"This is none other than the most magnificent merchandise." Approvingly Yusuf fingered the edges of some finely-forged blades.

"Only the finest blades from Damascus and Yemen do I display here. What is your desire?"

Yusuf picked out a broad, double-edged steel dagger-blade inlaid with gold at the top, admiring the raised spine bisecting it and running its full length. It curved slightly and tapered from the middle to a spiky point. Its silver-clad hilt was made of ivory with a T-shaped crown.

"The steel is superb and sharp enough to split a hair," the vendor boasted.

"Have you a sheath for this blade?"

"Yes, my lord." The vendor's hands scrambled among several scabbards spread upon the table before them until he picked one having a felt-lined leather belt, presenting it for inspection. Their fine muslin head cloths—each bound by double-coiled woolen circlets—almost butted as Yusuf held up the scabbard before their expectant eyes.

"Only the finest embossed steel adorns this scabbard," the vendor boasted. "Only the finest red cotton lines the inside."

"For what price will you sell this dagger and scabbard?"

"What price would you give me?"

"For how much will you sell them?" Yusuf persisted.

"Are you one of the People of the Pact," an appealing feminine voice abruptly interrupted their haggling, "the unbelieving subjects protected by the caliphate?"

Yusuf turned about to look where the voice came from and found standing close to him a lone, well-formed woman wrapped up in a long black cloak embroidered with gold metal thread. She lifted up her eyes from beneath her delicately embroidered white gauze veil, encrusted on front and back with silver metal thread.

"I'm a freedman whose master has died." He looked curiously into her dark, languorous and long-lashed eyes. "What about you? Should you be roaming the streets alone or do you not fear arrest?"

"My sister waits for me nearby."

"Do you wish then to help me choose a dagger?" He nodded sideways towards the blade vendor who was figuring the dagger's value upon the palm of his hand. "My merchant friend is anxious to take his price for the dagger. What do you think it's worth?"

"My mistress will buy for you the dagger at whatever price," she said.

"Your mistress?" Yusuf looked puzzled. "Why should she do me this favor?"

"My mistress bids you to perform for her a service for which she will richly reward you, but only if you can perform it quickly and discreetly as one of few words."

"What service might that be?"

"She has need of someone to carry to her house a basket which is too heavy for her sisters to bear."

"Surely," Yusuf smiled, "if your mistress can buy a stranger a dagger she can afford to hire herself a porter."

"Of course. She can afford to hire many porters. Only she proposes to offer you much more for your services than mere gold."

"You intrigue me, my sister. Just how much more does she offer?"

"What would you say to a handsome house with running water, fruit and wine," her brilliantly black eyes flashed above her rouged cheeks and her brass wrist-bracelets clinked as she clasped her hands and lightly nudged Yusuf's chest with two touching fingers, "a beautiful face to behold, a smooth cheek to kiss, a shapely form to embrace—and to enjoy all these sumptuous pleasures and delights without restraint or interruption?"

"You tempt me, my sister." Yusuf looked skeptical. "How is it that you have searched me out in preference to all the men of Baghdad for this wonderful duty?"

"Did I not tell you had to be one of few words?"

"Why do you hesitate, man?" The merchant stared, looking baffled. "What restrains you? Watch over my shop for me and I will happily go in your place."

"As one very wise and learned man has said," Yusuf answered tellingly, pausing momentarily to consider the matter further, "it is highly advisable to do the exact opposite of anything any woman might propose."

Both the woman and the shopkeeper watched him expectantly.

"Very well," Yusuf heaved a resigned sigh, holding up his palms in unresisting surrender. "I volunteer myself in your lady's service as a man of few words. Where is this basket of yours?"

"My sister stands over it close by." She bowed slightly with assent. "Be silent and come with me."

"I hear and obey," Yusuf said willingly. "Go before me and lead the way."

Suddenly the shopkeeper grabbed his arm and held fast before he could leave.

"You will remember to come back and buy the dagger with your reward?"

"Without fail," Yusuf grinned knowingly, "but not—I hope—before the time of the dawn prayer draws near."

Yusuf went after the woman as she shuffled off ahead of him, treading her path in her stitched-canvas sandals. He reveled in watching her remarkable gait—gracefully sidling her lower hips back and forth while holding tight to her bosom the edges of her outer cloak. She stared down only at the ground in the direction she was walking. He followed her out of the bazaar to the entrance of a nearby side street by which another woman, cloaked and veiled much the same as she was, stood reservedly waiting. Next to her stood a tall, sturdy-looking reed basket to which the woman leading him pointed.

"Take up this basket and follow us," she commanded.

"By God's good grace I will," he consented.

When Yusuf stooped to take up the basket he found it was so ponderous he could barely budge it without overexerting himself. Annoyed he lifted up his eyes to the two women.

"What you need to bear this burden is a pack mule—not a porter," he scoffed. "Where is your house, my sister?"

"Before us and there remains only a short distance to it," she scowled.

"There is no strength nor power but in God, the High, the Great!" Yusuf exclaimed.

"Up with it and follow us," she challenged him, "or are you a weakling?"

"I have nothing of strength to prove to you, my sister," he defied her. "What have you in this basket?"

"I told you…"

"I know," he cut her short and stood firm to lay a firmer hold on the basket, "I'm supposed to be a man of few words. I only pray you won't mind a few grunts."

"This is no time for idle wit or complaint," she stood indignantly firm. "Just lift and follow us."

"Hearing is obeying, my sister," he strained with all his might to heave the basket upon his shoulder, buckling beneath its weight and groaning. "Lead on, my sister. Just make haste, I implore you!"

Again he marveled at the sidling gait of both women as they shuffled on ahead of him.

"Remarkable," he admiringly murmured to himself, "truly remarkable!"

Together they plodded along several of the quarter's narrow and dusty back streets—all lined with keel-arched doorways and overhung with jutting balconies. Before long they came to a double-leafed ebony gate inlaid with plates of red gold, silver and ultramarine over which was inscribed the verse:

A pleasing mansion to every guest when to him all others displease.

Unlocking an iron padlock with their key the two women noiselessly budged aside the gate's twin leaves so Yusuf could awkwardly hobble into the long and dark passage opening up into a central courtyard at its far end.

"Put down your burden," the woman commanded him.

"Gladly!" he heaved a relieved sigh as he plunked the basket down onto the ground.

"Now wait for us outside while we inform our mistress of our safe return home." She gestured for him to seat himself on a stone bench built along the front of the manor-house. Yusuf shrugged and obediently plunked himself down onto the raised stone seat.

"Move not from this spot until I return to you."

Then the women passed behind the door-leaves, pushed and barred them shut with a clang.

Once he sat down and rested, wincing up at the blazing sun above, Yusuf felt his sweat beading profusely upon his skin and soaking into his long, cream cotton body-shirt. He undid the tasseled tie-cords at the banded neckline of his gold and silver trimmed outer cloak, threw it off his shoulders and draped it across the bench. He unbuttoned his shirt's high and round-banded collar and slid open the frontal slit reaching to his middle chest. Then he stood up, wiping with his large open sleeve the sweat oozing from his grimacing face and forehead.

Examining more closely the mansion's twin-leafed gate Yusuf saw protruding from each doorplate a fearsome looking brass figure—a bull's head—each one bordered at its neck in aquamarine with knocker rings hanging from each of their noses. Then suddenly he heard window shutters creak open above him and he looked up. Looking down over him was yet another white-skinned, oval-faced and dark-eyed woman wearing a silken headscarf fringed and tasseled in azure blue. For a moment she paused to gaze down upon him and then leaned out over the window sill, holding a row of small encased potted plants, and reached out to dangle in the air a small piece of colored cloth. Finally she let the cloth go to flutter down for him to catch and then retired from sight. What Yusuf caught was a plain, silken, oblong handkerchief embroidered with red gold. He flattened it over his palm and found stitched into its fabric a red gold design in the very same image of the doorplate figures: a forbidding bull's head. Again he looked up at the window but the woman was gone. Then he heard scuffing footsteps trudging up slowly and abrasively from behind. Yusuf turned about to see an old woman wearing a white calico cloak and leaning upon a rattan cane limp up to him, reaching out in front of herself with her free hand to feel her way.

"Alms, for the love of Allah!" she begged.

Sensing her nearness to him she stopped but a step away from him.

"What do you desire?" Yusuf asked her.

43

"I desire something for the sake of God—whose name be exalted!—for I am in need of the mercy of God."

"Know that I would give you the blood of my heart. Are you blind?"

"Yes."

"Then give me your hand."

Yusuf took her free hand in his while reaching into his waist belt pocket.

"Prayer carries us halfway to Allah," she said. "Fasting brings us to the door of His palace. And alms moves us to step through His gate." As Yusuf gently pressed a coin into her palm the old beggar woman smiled her gratitude. "The generous is the friend of Allah although he may be a sinner. And the miser is the enemy of Allah although he may be a saint. What is your name, my son?"

"Yusuf."

"This is one of the names of kings. Are you of this country?"

"I am a citizen. But I was born of another country."

"It is of no importance." She grabbed and squeezed his hand tightly, pleading. "I beg that you will walk with me a few paces so that I may tell you something."

"I hear and obey. But I cannot go far from here. Go before me."

Yusuf offered her his arm to lean upon. They walked only a few steps toward the middle of the street before the old woman turned to him and looked up at his face with her searching, sightless eyes.

"O my son," her tone turned desperate, "may God—whose name be exalted!—preserve you and grant you the enjoyment of your youth, for I pray for you the protection of the Lord of the Dawn!"

"Protection from what?"

"From the craft and cunning of the scheming woman of that house, for cunning as a serpent she is!"

"You mean the house outside which I was waiting?"

"Yes."

"Who is the woman of that house?"

"How is it that you do not know her when you have been in her company?"

"I have not been in her company yet. We have yet to meet."

"May Allah—whose name be exalted!—destroy her!" the old woman's flaccid cheeks quivered as she prattled. "Surely there lives and breathes no woman more treacherous and deceitful than she! How many men she has slaughtered before you—and what vile deeds she has done—cannot be counted!"

"My aunt, who acquainted you with her?"

"My son, I may be blind but I am not unseeing. I know her as the age knows its calamities."

"Praise be to God who has made me acquainted with you! But I still must go and take my reward for a service I performed."

"No, by Allah! You will take no reward from that evil house. I beg you to stay well away from there!"

Suddenly they heard the bar of the manor-house's gate unbolt. Together the two turned but only Yusuf could see the veiled woman from the bazaar standing between the cracked door-leaves.

"My brother!" she called out to Yusuf. "My mistress salutes you and summons you to be her guest."

"May God avert from you the wickedness of the blood-thirsty!" The old woman clamped around his right wrist a silver-gray metal bracelet of tiny bells before he could answer back.

"What is this?"

"A talisman to ward off evil, for a wicked woman is an arrow of the Devil."

"May Allah open up to you another door of generosity, my pilgrim." He warmly pressed her purple-veined hand in gratitude.

"Take care, my son. Remember this saying should you have

45

need of it, for it was no accident that when the Prophet stood at the gate of Hell most of the captives he saw were women: *fidelity is good and treachery is base!*"

Smiling Yusuf left the old woman to accost the maiden of the manor-house.

"Go to your mistress and salute her for me with abundant salutations and tell her I am at her service to command as she will."

"Enter now to answer her summons, for she expects you."

She waved him inside and barred the gate shut when Yusuf stepped into the long and dark narrow passage leading to the central courtyard.

"My mistress again bids you welcome," she advised him. "She became enamored of you when she looked upon your face from the window and longs for you to pass the night with her. And if you act agreeably you will see prosperity and good fortune."

"Never in my life have I seen a day more fortunate or blessed than this!" he smiled dubiously, clutching at the bracelet to keep the bells from clinking. "I hear and obey."

"Good. Wait here with the basket while I go and tell my mistress you have accepted her invitation, for her longing for you consumes her." She scurried off down the long, dark and narrow passage, disappearing around a corner and into the distant and indistinct courtyard.

Yusuf was left standing alone in the shadowy passage and staring down at the palm-stick basket standing next to him. Burning with curiosity he craved to look and see what was contained so weightily within and could resist no longer the temptation to find out. So slowly he slid and pried off the basket-lid beckoning him. Laid bare before him was the limp body of a man curled up in the cramped bottom of the basket and bundled up in a blue worker's smock. He looked alive, barely breathing but leaden. Yusuf reached down to feel the slightly pulsating warmth of the man's throat and then, suddenly, everything blurred and grew black before his eyes. He crumpled senseless to the dusty ground as glinting gold showed in the grinning teeth of the burly black eunuch who stepped up into the hallway's lamplight—brandishing the short-handled steel mace with the bull-shaped head with which he had just walloped the nape of Yusuf's neck.

When Yusuf awoke, writhing and groping for the shooting pain at the nape of his neck—the tiny bells tinkling at his wrist—he found his head cloth gone and then felt for his throbbing forehead. When he moved he felt like he was lying upon a billowing, undulating and meandering bed-quilt. As he strained to focus his eyes he found he was lying beneath a silken coverlet upon a wide couch overlaid with a bouncy, buoyant-feeling satin mattress tethered securely by taut bands of silk—each band cross-tied to four ringed pegs of pure silver anchored at each corner. He stripped aside part of the coverlet and ran his palm slowly over the springy surface.

"Quicksilver," the familiar feminine voice said.

Yusuf thrashed and twisted beneath his coverlet to look behind to find the woman from the bazaar hovering over him, gently waving above him a palm-stick fan of neatly-woven black ostrich feathers.

"What?" he looked disbelieving.

"The bed of skins you're lying upon rests upon a pool of quicksilver. The rippling sensation is believed to ease and deepen your slumber. And you slept most peacefully."

"Sleeping was easy enough." He arched his eyebrows and bulged his eyes. "It was waking which was difficult. So who do I compliment for helping me sleep so soundly?"

"One of the guards of the house. He disapproved of your looking at what did not concern you. And whoever in this house looks at what does not concern him knows no delight."

"You speak truly," Yusuf affirmed. "Tell me, my sister, what might I look at which could cause me delight? Your lovely face perhaps? Why don't you unveil it for me so that I might take delight in it?"

"My brother presumes to take too much upon himself too soon." Her eyes looked perturbed. "You shall take your delight here no doubt—but not without cost."

"Truly, but when?"

"Right now."

She put down her fan, stood up and lifted the netted curtain screening in the couch to lay open before them a large octagonal saloon-apartment with gypsum-plastered and whitewashed walls and wooden-lattice windows, above which were smaller windows of colored glass.

"My brother," she said ceremoniously, "we have a mind to do you honor and would happily have you enter our chamber and share in our entertainment and merriment, and so cheer our hearts."

"So be it," Yusuf sat up with a groan upon the edge of the watery bed groping his nape.

"Come and take your fill of food and drink."

"Take me," he stood up sluggishly to take the full measure of the room.

He stood upon a platform elevated some half a foot above the rest of the carpeted stone floor, paved with white and black marble, inlaid tastefully with intricately patterned red tiles, and stretching to a door at the opposite wall. In the middle of the floor stood a jetting fountain which spouted into a small, shallow pool, afloat with tinkling glass bells and paved and lined with colored marbles. Ahead the woman stepped down and gestured for him to seat himself upon another thick, cotton-stuffed, calico-covered mattress set upon a raised frame against a wall.

"Take your ease here," she told him. "Wait a little and you will gain your desire."

"How long will I wait before I gain it?"

"When my mistress has become exhilarated with wine you will gain her favor."

Obediently Yusuf sat down upon a low-lying mattress and rested himself against its velvet-embroidered cushions and pillows filled with ostrich down.

"By God," he smoothed his palm over one of the velvet-covered cushions, "this must be either a piece of Paradise or some king's palace!"

"You are welcome and your day is blessed!"

With a slight bow she left the room through the far door. All at once several comely, young and unveiled maidservants carried in the table-service together with coal-fired, globular-shaped censers burning aromatic ambergris, musk and aloes-wood, setting these to blend with the sweet-smelling scents of tall jars holding narcissus, roses, violets and other flowers. Upon a short stool, sitting upon a round embroidered floor-cloth, they set a large round silver tray inlaid with mother-of-pearl and ebony, upon which were set golden platters and gilded porcelain dishes piled with small cuts of roasted and butter-cooked lamb, mutton and fowl, sausages, stewed vegetables, cucumbers, along with cabbage and lettuce leaves stuffed with minced meat and rice.

One servant girl handed Yusuf a napkin before she poured scented rose-water over his hands and into a basin from a gilded brass bottle, a spherical ewer with a long and narrow neck, followed by another who brought him a porcelain bowl of clear meat-and-vegetable soup.

"Welcome to you, my brother. Eat so that the bond of bread and salt may be made between us."

From a tall woman wearing a long robe brocade with a gold-embroidered hem, standing silhouetted in the threshold of the doorway at the opposite wall, came an alluring feminine voice. As she stepped forward into the lamplight her robe rippled when her hips sidled to and fro in a graceful, swaying gait. As she drew near she raised the azure veil from her oval-white face, parting her coral-red lips and smiling seductively, showing her pearly-white teeth.

"You wish to obligate me to you?" Yusuf sat erect to feast his eyes upon her.

She stepped up close by and dropped her robe at his bare feet, showing an apricot-colored chemise-shift hanging loosely and straight from her shoulders. Her firm, upright breasts swelled like two evenly-shaped pomegranates standing wide apart and facing outward from one another. Her stomach fell in supple waves and tapered to her slender waist and wide hips. Exposed below her short slip where her thickset but smooth white thighs. She sat right down upon the mattress next to him and leaned forward close to him, gazing into his face with her dark, languishing and kohl-lined eyes. Long silken lashes deepened even more her half-closed eyelids.

"I wish to unite you to me."

With her right hand she reached and drew a delicate square morsel of lamb from the edge of a platter and touched it gently to Yusuf's lips.

"Eat and do not be ashamed, for I know you suffer from the violence of your hunger."

Yusuf took the offered morsel upon his tongue, gently nibbling it off her henna-stained fingertips.

"In the name of God..." he started.

"The Compassionate, the Merciful," she finished.

Abruptly she clapped her left palm with the fingers of her right hand and a young maidservant appeared from the adjoining room.

"Bring the wine and fruits," she commanded and the girl immediately left.

"You take the forbidden drink?"

"Do you think me wicked for it?" she smiled impishly.

"It is written that wine is the source of more evil than good and compels men to do only the Devil's work."

She set both her palms upon the mattress astride Yusuf's legs and leaned over upon her arms closer to him—an essence of jasmine filtering up to his nostrils. Then she suddenly shook her long and full black hair—her long tresses carelessly fringing her soft face in loose, curling ringlets.

"Do I look like an evil woman or a demon?" she leered at him, open-mouthed.

"More like the graceful willow—or a temptress perhaps—but a hungry woman to be sure."

Suddenly the young maidservant reappeared bringing the wine-service and, her mistress dismissing her with a curt wave of her hand, she bowed and left again. Into a crystal goblet gilded with silver and gold the woman paused to pour wine from a flagon.

"Give me your right arm," she commanded.

As Yusuf held out his right arm—so she could drape a richly-embroidered napkin over it upon which he could wipe his lips after drinking—the tiny bracelet-bells tinkled.

"You've been talking to that meddling old blind woman who roams our streets accosting our guests and callers, I see," she scowled.

"She warned me you were a wicked woman," Yusuf admitted with a smirk.

"Take this cup," she offered him the goblet, "for it will delight you."

"Should not you drink first?" he hesitated.

"What ails you?" she glared at him sardonically. "Do you think it is poisoned? And will not your silly bells protect you from it if it is?"

Yusuf merely raised his eyebrows and shrugged.

"This is an excellent cordial," she boasted, "which cheers the heart and enlivens the spirits. By our custom I will show you."

She drank off the entire cup, calmly poured another and again offered it to him.

"By my life take this cup," she held it up to his lips, "this giver of joy to which reason surrenders, and may it be attended by health and vitality."

"Happily I will drink it from your hand," he covered her

hands with his own.

He drained it, savoring its sweet and thick flavor.

"There," she said, satisfied, "wine is as the body, music as the soul and joy is their offspring."

Then she clapped again and yet another comely young maidservant appeared, kneeling and bowing as she sat down upon her cloaked haunches, holding carefully in her lap a short-necked, pear-shaped lute.

"Shariyya," the woman commanded her, "go to your closet and play."

Without ever looking up the servant girl adjusted her lute's four frets and gently plucked their strings with an eagle's feather. Then she bowed, rose and stepped up into an elevated recess across the room, retiring behind a screen of wooden lattice-work. Soon the sweet tone of her lute flowed from behind the screen and filled the air with its soft, slow, sensuous and mournfully melodious sounds.

"Do you enjoy the song of the lute?" the woman asked Yusuf.

"Exceedingly."

"It is said that Lamak made the very first lute from the leg of his own dead son whose loss he mourned with it."

Yusuf looked upon her longingly.

"It is also said," she reached over to undo the neckline tassel of Yusuf's body-shirt, "that music and song help untangle the knots of the soul and make men see the beauty of their universe."

"I see your beauty," he said.

For a fleeting moment they were both conspicuously and profoundly quiet, and then Yusuf reached for her soft and rounded upper arms, gently caressing them. She looked upon him searchingly.

"Do I tempt you?" she smiled mischievously, reaching herself for a yellow flower from a nearby chinaware vessel, holding it up between his grasping arms—first to her own nose and then to his—letting him smell of it. "This gilliflower is a sign of a neglected lover, for that is what I am." She laid it down upon the mattress beside them.

"Your words are doubtful. What do you really desire?"

Again she reached and took a piece of banana from a small dish and dipped it into a saucer of honey before holding it up to Yusuf's lips, breathlessly watching him chew off a piece and swallow it.

"The Prophet said the banana-tree is the only thing of earth which looks like a thing of Paradise." She put down the rest of the fruit and looked back into Yusuf's eyes—her hands parting the front slit of his body-shirt, her palms caressing the hair of his chest. "I desire that you taste my honey and enter into my paradise!"

"With love and gladness."

Their breaths and pulses quickened, hot blood surging through their bodies as her mouth came down greedily upon his. Frantically she tugged at the bottom of his body-shirt and pushed the folds above his hips all the way up to his armpits as she mounted him, kneeling astride his legs and then wriggling down over him to brush his chest with her breasts. At the same time he had fallen back upon the mattress raising her silken shift above her own hips. Higher she climbed upon him as he firmly gripped her hips, guiding her to him until they joined.

"Impale me!" she gasped. "Invade me!"

Burning fire had seethed into his vitals and she sat up erect, arching her back and uttering a shrill cry as he penetrated her. Warm and sappy liquid gushed profusely out of her and melted down upon him with a stinging, burning heat. He reached up to her with both hands, caressing her flushed, ruddy cheeks, running them down along her sleek and smooth throat, and then farther down over her firm, uprising breasts until his fingers passed over her soft belly and pierced her wide hollow navel. As frenzied as the lute music then trilled their fervid, heaving bodies rubbed together, undulating, and fumed.

Without warning a swimming dizziness stunned Yusuf's senses and struck him senseless. His head spinned, feeling numb and emptied. His vision blurred and the gold-corniced ceiling hovering high above him was suddenly clouded over and blacked out by several fearsome bull's faces staring down menacingly upon him, overshadowed in murky, reddish hues—and light became darkness before his eyes.

§

"Open your eyes!" Yusuf heard the commaning voice of the seductress fall abruptly upon his ears.

Pinned down at his arms and legs by four burly black slaves he felt riveted to the carpet he was lying immovably upon. He inhaled a pungent odor as the seductress bent over him wafting a burning aromatic lozenge back and forth under his nose.

"Which of the two states is more pleasing to you, dearest," she asked mockingly, "life or death?"

"My life, your death," he scoffed.

"You insolent dog!" she cried contemptuously. "As a reward for your gullibility I shall slaughter you as the goats are slaughtered!"

"My sister," he cut her short, "you do truly serve abundant and pleasing entertainment. But who are you that I might repay you for your hospitality?"

"You fool! Far be it from me that what has happened should happen again or that I should ever be in your company after this time?"

"Why so, my sister?" he feigned regret. "I had hoped we would join night and day together, although truly I must go my way before morning."

Suddenly she held up before his eyes a glinting, gilded blade.

"I am the Daughter of Delilah!" she announced, her clenched teeth grinding. "And I will surely slaughter you with this knife—the dagger I promised you! Lay bare his throat!" One of her slaves clutched his hair, wrenching his head back violently.

"Fidelity is good and treachery is base!" Yusuf groaned, grimacing in fear.

"So," the seductress looked suddenly resigned and defeated, "you have spared your life from me through the help of these words. By Allah I must cause you to bear a mark of my resentment. But first hasten to give me one last kiss."

Again she bent down and covered his mouth ravenously with her own, abruptly stood up, and firmly and resolutely slashed a clean incision into his upper left chest. Blood seeped instantly from the wound and Yusuf lapsed once more into deep unconsciousness.

"Sell him to the galleys!" the Daughter of Delilah blurted out bitterly.

THREE:
DIVER OF PEARL

COURSERS

"By the snorting war steeds, which strike fire with their hoofs as they gallop to the raid at dawn and with a trail of dust split the foe in two; man is ungrateful to his Lord! To this he himself shall bear witness."—Surah C

As Yusuf's thoughts returned to the present he heard himself cry out from the piercing pain of the knife wound and felt himself fingering the red scar gashed across his left chest.

"The honey the temptress fed me was laced with henbane," Yusuf recalled, "the poisonous herb which disorders the mind and reason, and put me at her mercy. And so I fell prey to her treachery and came to grief. And now I have come to you in this place."

"Praise be to God that she did not slaughter you!" Fatima exclaimed. "By God, my son, you have truly been miraculously preserved! Were not the term of your life a long one you would not have escaped from these straits, but would have died a violent death. But praised be God for your safety and protection, for the Lord has granted you new life!"

"Surely we are God's and to Him we are returning!" Yusuf affirmed. "But did you know I was coming to you here at this hour?"

"No. I did not know. Why do you ask?"

"I met a man on the doomed galley ship who described to me this—your place—and told me to go to you and salute you. And so I came in obedience to his command."

"Who was this man?"

"He claimed to have been a messenger sent from God. Only now he has been admitted to the mercy of God, whose name be exalted!"

"Praised be God! Praised be the Creator of all things, the Giver of daily bread, the Maker of the heavens and the Spreader of the earths!" Fatima professed, lifting up her eyes, her hands and her heart to the heavens. Then she looked upon Yusuf solemnly. "My son, everything you have experienced in this absence from your country—all the trials and ordeals you have suffered and endured—all these things are appointed by the Almighty, for as the Prophet has said: *Whatever is in the universe is by the order of God.* Know also that had you not happened here you would have perished miserably and no one would have known of you ever again. But I will be the means of saving your life and of returning you to your fatherland."

"How will this be done, my aunt? I hardly feel I know my fatherland anymore."

"Put your trust in God and confide your case to Him, the Lord who made mankind," she counseled. "Quit your fear and be content of mind. Ask nothing of the past or how or why it came to pass, for all things are by fate and destiny designed."

"My aunt," Yusuf said appreciatively, "you have been the means of my deliverance from the hand of sudden death and I am beholden to you for it. How can I repay your kindness?"

"You owe me nothing so you need repay me nothing. When we find a man shipwrecked upon our shore we take him up and give him food and drink. Nor do we take anything from him. We simply treat him kindly and graciously for the love of God the Most High. And…"

Fatima started to say something else but paused as if she remembered something important.

"Yes, my aunt?" Yusuf watched her smile mirthfully.

"And if he is naked," she continued, assuming an amused but emphatic attitude, "we clothe him."

Mortified Yusuf stared down at his bare black loincloth.

"Perhaps my aunt's deep devotion to piety and prayer has made her forgetful," he smiled unabashedly.

"You are already shorn," Fatima scolded him, scowling. "Do not be shameless as well."

She gestured to a large high-backed, canopy-covered chair of cane-work sitting nearby upon the open-air terrace-floor with a body-shirt and cloak draped over it, along with sandals at its feet.

"Put on this dress, Yusuf, and welcome to you!"

"Are you sure you did not expect me?"

Yusuf slipped smoothly into the long cream cotton body-shirt with braid and piping, which had large open sleeves, side

60

panels with inset pockets and vertical slits opening at each side. Its neckline was high, round and had a banded collar with a buttoned opening at the studded shirt-front reaching to the middle chest. Gold-embroidered and trimmed the cream-colored cloak also had a banded neckline terminating in two small decorative, tasseled tie-cords.

"My aunt," he draped himself in the cloak, "where is this place—this land—and who are its people if it has any?"

"You have landed upon the island known to us as the Isle of Pearl," Fatima told him, watching him step into the stitched canvas sandals, "which lies secluded in the outermost oceans of the world. Very few men know or have even heard of its existence. Later we will speak much more of this at our leisure. For now I bid you to descend back to the seashore and wait in our Harbor of Safe Refuge until I summon you again."

"Harbor of Safe Refuge?"

"Yes. It is a special place we preserve for weary and way-worn travelers such as yourself."

"It is free of the deadly stallion sentinels?"

"Of course."

"How do I alight there? The mountain is high and the way down is perilous. And surely the great Roc bird wearies of carrying me."

"A woman of pure Arabian blood will carry you," Fatima smiled knowingly, amused at Yusuf's mystified expression. "Come with me."

Yusuf followed Fatima the Devotee through the shadowy mosque gallery and out into the open-air part of the transverse forecourt. She sauntered and stood close to the five chestnut-colored statues of five Arabian horses standing majestically at the edge of the courtyard fountain—its quiet reflecting pool mirroring their glimmering images together with those of the tall colonnades encircling them—its trickling water barely audible.

"There is a wondrous story I wish to tell you."

"Tell me your tale, my aunt." Yusuf listened intently.

"It has been told," Fatima recounted, "how the Prophet—Mohammed—once penned up his horses without food or drink for three days and then set them free. Parched with thirst the horses headed straight for the nearest water hole. But Mohammed ordered the horn of battle to be sounded—the signal for all noble war horses to return to camp and prepare for fighting. With mouths as dry as the desert winds most of the mares ignored the call and kept on moving toward the water hole. Only five loyal mares turned about in their tracks and returned all at once. Since obedience was the quality Mohammed valued most in his horses these five mares took his blessing. From that time on they were called—one and all—the five mares of the Prophet. And they came to be the source of all pure Arabian blood. And their direct descendants were the only horses so favored to bear the name *Asil*—or pureblood. Have you ever heard anything like this story?"

"Surely this is an excellent story," Yusuf declared, "but what importance do you attach to it?"

"I will show you," Fatima stooped to reach her hand into the brimming pool, taking up from it a handful of water. "Tradition tells how God took a handful of the south wind and created from it a golden horse of chestnut color and said to it, *I have created you and named you Arab.*"

Droplets of water fell from her upturned palm and pattered onto the hard flagstone floor as she strolled over to one of the bay mare statues poised regally with the left front leg raised and the right rear leg slightly stepping. Gently she raised her cupped hand to the mare's stone lips, wetting them with water as if she expected her to drink.

"And God said," Fatima continued, "I have given you My blessing over all the other beasts and made you their master. Good fortune is bound to your forelock. Bounty rests upon your back and in your loins. And prosperity will be with you wherever you may go."

She stood off and well clear of the statue as it suddenly glowed with a gleaming bluish violet shimmer of lapis lazuli, coursing its way throughout its entire stone body, radiating and shooting out beams of bright, luminescent light. Yusuf was taken aback and held up his hands to shield his eyes from the light's dazzling, blinding brilliance.

"And God said," Fatima continued, "I have empowered you to fly without wings, for you are bound for flight and pursuit. And you will carry men who will glorify Me, and by them you will glorify Me."

Just as suddenly the blazing, bluish bay horse became animated and began to move—alive and lively—slowly at first and then more actively and vivaciously—struggling to breathe, whinny, rear up upon her hind legs and assume the form of a living thing!

"There is no Majesty and there is no Might except in God, the Glorious, the Great!" Yusuf exclaimed, looking aghast.

After clopping at the air with her front hoofs the beautiful bay Arabian mare settled down and strutted proudly but gracefully right over to Fatima, who took into both her hands the horse's fine-boned cheeks, caressing them affectionately.

"What is the secret of this horse and her animation?" Yusuf asked, lost in amazement.

"God gives the earth water and by it gives life," she said simply, looking lovingly into the mare's lovely dished face.

Soon the mare's scintillant blue light faded and slowly melted away from her stately, spirited body. Then only her eyes flashed with fiery light.

"Come closer and salute her," Fatima softly stroked the fine and supple coat of her highly-held arched neck.

"Magnificent!" Yusuf exclaimed, awestruck, as he stepped up to softly stroke the bay mare's deep, shining and smooth-muscled chest.

"My son," Fatima told him, "if ever you mount this horse your mind and reason will be confounded."

"How so, my aunt?"

"My son, the profound secret of this horse is that if you mount her she will carry you, take to the air and fly with you wherever you wish to wander or roam. And through the air she can cross the space of a whole year in a single day!"

"Unbelievable!" Yusuf exclaimed, struck with wonder.

"For now she will be the means of your traveling back to the shore of the sea."

"What do these words mean, my aunt?"

"In time this Arabian mare may help you gain your desire," she answered. "Mount her."

Obediently Yusuf mounted the horse's bare back and clenched her long and glossy mane.

"My desire is still much in doubt," he confessed.

"He who does not risk himself will never gain his desire," she admonished him. "Beyond this I cannot yet tell, but this night I will pray and implore God to be rightly directed about the course you must pursue."

Slowly and smoothly the mare stepped upwards and started to rise with her rider into the air, casting a looming shadow over the watchful woman standing below them—the ground gradually dropping away from beneath them, the surrounding colonnades sinking past them until they were underfoot!

"Where will I go and what will I do?" Yusuf cried out anxiously, spellbound as he watched Fatima, straining her eyes to look up at him, slip away and shrink in size.

"You will go back to the seashore," she answered urgently, "and you will learn to pray!"

§

As the swift and sturdy Arabian mare arose and sprang higher and higher into the shining, bright blue sky Yusuf affectionately caressed and leaned closer to her satiny coated neck, staring down breathlessly at the expansive ocean spreading out far below them. Soon he could see—lying in the middle of the vast, deep blue water—the entire enchanted isle.

Submerged sea cliffs rose abruptly and precipitously from the ocean all around, soaring skyward and culminating in the flattened peak of a great submarine summit resting upon craggy volcanic rocks. Atop and across the island's spacious crown stretched its expansive central plateau, which fell to the sea on all sides in descending terraces broken up by steep slopes and sheer cliffs. Overlying the plateau surface were shallow valleys and conical, flat-topped hills hemmed in by a raised rim of jagged limestone pinnacles. Showing through the shallower blue water surrounding the base of the island lay a fringing coral reef. On top of the loftiest escarpment of the deeply fissured sea cliff Yusuf saw Fatima's dwindling celestial shrine standing upon its towering terrace at the very brink of the shoreless sea. At the center of the mosque roof he saw a golden, glinting dome topped by a radiant but indistinct figure, which by squinting he could make out only obscurely.

Gusty warm winds whipped and waved across the mare's fine silken mane and whisked through Yusuf's hair as she gently descended and easily alighted onto the soft white shingle sands of a crescent-shaped beach, jutting out at the land's edge from a spacious and quiet cove. Yusuf dismounted her as soon as her hoofs touched the ground and appreciatively caressed her proudly arched neck in gratitude.

"You have done well, my beauty!" he praised her. "Take no offense, but I wish your mistress had sent you to me for the ascent as well."

Almost in assent the magnificent mare briskly nodded her head, pranced smartly and bounded into the air again, rising higher up the face of the surrounding sea cliffs and passing over their sky-reaching ridge until she was lost to sight.

Encircled on all sides by soaring sea cliffs the peaceful horseshoe-shaped cove Yusuf stood upon emptied its beach into the still, sheltered sea waters, fringed beyond offshore by a narrow coral reef. Tumbling down in a gushing cascade from over the ridge of a side cliff a long, spewing waterfall plunged and plummeted into a narrow stream running along the foot of the cliff, cutting across the beach's edge and emptying alongside it into the ocean. Beneath and behind the spraying and splashing falls a gaping, cavernous grotto opened up at the mouth of the bordering stream, from which the running waters ebbed and flowed with the tides.

Nearby stood a long, low and flat black Arabian tent. Prudently Yusuf stepped up to admire the loose weave of its thick, heavily worsted woolen cloth, stretched over upright poles and staked by very long stays made of hemp. Tension bands were sewn across the wide cloth breadths so the ropes, attached by wooden block stay-fasteners, pulled tautly across the seams. He could see daylight through the cloth and found the tent completely open—propped by a small, circular wooden plaque of a ridgepole—so the hot sea air could blow throughout. Inside the tent he could see woven bag and bent-wood chest containers set upon rugs, mats and shaggy woolen carpets dyed Turkey red. Wall curtains made of a looser weave, and woven with red and brick geometric designs, were hung from the ropes forming a variety of inner enclosures. Another dividing curtain, a carpet dyed scarlet, separated men's and women's quarters. By custom Yusuf approached the tent from the front and saw no one about, although he found a small burning hearth of three stones, crisscrossed with iron bars, set just outside the tent and bearing a kettle of boiling water. Goat-skin water bags lay nearby and a wooden tripod suspended a goatskin churn.

Beyond the tent Yusuf moved toward the magnificent waterfall looming ahead. For a long time he stood admiring the long cascade crashing down upon the running stream below, flying with spray and mist, before strolling along the water's edge, feeling refreshed from breathing in the cool wetness filling the air. Finally he sat down to rest and watch the rushing waters flow from the pool at the yawning mouth of the grotto, agitated and clouded by the tumbling falls.

Suddenly Yusuf heard another sound—the gurgle of bubbles! He stared down into the stream and saw the water ripple from bubbles percolating up from below—beneath the clear blue surface. Next he saw the faint, golden brown coloring of a blurred and hazy outline, a shadowy figure appearing and taking shape from below. Gradually the figure grew and gained flesh as it ascended the depths and drew nearer to the surface. Soon Yusuf could pick out the head and shoulders of a human being—a man! He was crawling up! Abruptly he burst up through the surface, water running off his cleanly shaven head, which was darkened only by the shade of his shorn hair. Lustily he snorted, blew out the rest of the air from his suppressed lungs and rubbed his bleary eyes. He plucked a horn clip from his nose and let it drop upon a string hung round his neck and then lifted up his eyes, his dark, joined brows and high forehead furrowing deeply. He gulped in a deep breath.

"Peace be with you, my son!" he gasped. "Lend me your hand."

"And on you be the peace of God and His blessing!" Yusuf braced his feet, reached down, grasped the man's up-reaching hand and pulled him out of the water. He stood aghast at the man, watching the water spill off his tall, lean and muscular bronzed body, naked except for a soaked black loincloth.

"Why do you look upon me so curiously?" the man asked him.

"I merely marvel at how you burst out from the water."

"Did you expect perhaps a maiden of the sea?"

"No, but you suggest a pleasurable prospect. Who are you?"

"My name is Malik. I am the master of my craft and I have no equal in this domain."

Respectfully they saluted one another.

"Welcome to you, my sheik," Yusuf greeted him. "What is your craft?"

"My son, we are here in this domain divers of pearls. We descend into the depths for precious pearls, and our calling is a difficult and dangerous one."

"Why have you come here to me?"

"To be your sheik and master."

"I am my own master," Yusuf frowned indignantly.

"My Yusuf," the man addressed him soothingly, "if you hope to survive and remain in this domain you are from this day forward my son. So call me nothing else other than your father and I will call you nothing else other than my son."

"My father is dead. And if you know my name, you also know I am an outsider here, and by trade a palace guard."

"You can never join the palace guard of this island," the man shook his head. "And we suffer no outsiders to be admitted into this our craft, which is strictly ordered. When one among us dies and departs this life we teach his son the craft. If he leaves no son we carry on deprived and missing one. And if he leaves two sons we teach one of them the craft. And if he dies we teach his brother. This our craft is strictly ordered."

"So you have said. What has this to do with me?"

"I merely tell you how here you may earn and gain your livelihood, and in what manner you will feel in your heart contented and at ease, for fear greed and idleness enter into you, and you aspire after what is not your condition."

"My only condition here is to take ship and get off this island so I may return to my fatherland."

"You speak truly, my son, but so very few ships ever find their way here to us, and we are so far away from any mainland shore that you could remain here with us for a very long time. Now tell me, from what place did you voyage and how came you into this island?"

"I was on a ship from Baghdad—one of the slave galleys—and it was wrecked and sank with all who were aboard her. But I got on a plank and landed here."

"Diving for pearls is the work of a galley slave," the man allowed, "for pearls lie in the heart of hot seas. It is a difficult and arduous quest full of obstacles and hardships. The treasures are lying there buried in their sunken caskets, and guarded by the currents and monsters of the sea. They must be pursued and searched for."

"Of what obstacles and hardships do you speak?"

"Heat, exhaustion and untold danger. Sea and sand burn under our sun. We dive in ancient fisheries with rocky bottoms, and we have plied our trade here for over a hundred years."

"Then you must dive for great destiny and good fortune."

"We dive not for profit or gain but for the love of God and His blessing!" the man exclaimed piously. "In His name and for His glory alone! But now I have need to tell you something more."

"Say on what you have to tell me."

"Behold!" Kneeling down over the sand Malik plowed an arc with his hand. "This is our prayer niche facing Mecca. Let us first pray together the midday prayer."

They kneeled side-by-side looking out upon the ocean, sprinkled their faces with sand in ablution, prostrated themselves and kissed the ground between their hands.

"God is great! God is great!" they chanted together in unison and then got up facing each other.

"You are a guest sent by God," Malik hailed him. "Enter this tent, then, that we might talk more together, and do not be afraid."

Together they stepped inside the tent and sat down upon the rug around the small fire. Kettle water still boiled over it. Rhythmically beating a stone pestle Malik pulverized skillet-roasted coffee beans in a heavy brass mortar. Next he poured the powder into a long-beaked copper pot along with boiling water and then set the pot on the fire to boil up again. Then he ground cardamom seeds in the mortar and added those to the coffee, smiling—satisfied—at his progress, his big white teeth gleaming brightly, his face beaming proudly.

"Even here we practice the ways of the desert," Malik affirmed.

Then he passed to Yusuf a platter of dates to take from.

"By Allah, you must eat!" he insisted, attentively watching Yusuf bite into the fresh fruit. "The Prophet has said: Honor your paternal aunt, the date-palm, for she was created of the earth of which Adam was formed."

Before long Malik tasted the coffee for flavor and looked pleased. Holding the pot in his left hand, and two tiny porcelain cups in his right, he filled each cup about one quarter full and held out both to his guest. From his outstretched hand Yusuf took one and together they drank.

"Sinbad, the great sailor of the sea," Malik recounted, "likened the pearl to fame and glory as the reward for toil and trouble and courage. Trouble, he reputedly said, makes fame more glorious once it is won since man's glory is the immortal daughter of many long nights spent without sleep!" He sipped his coffee and leaned upon his crossed legs. "He who would find the unsurpassed riches of the pearls of the sea must become a laboring galley slave before winning their glories. He who would win glory without toil and trouble will live a forlorn hope all his days!"

"That I would now trade one galley master for another is almost inconceivable," Yusuf said, pointing with wonder at Malik's sunburned breast. "What of that amulet which hangs about your neck?"

"I wear it to help protect me from the perils of the deep." Malik thumbed the silver disc pendant strung with his nose-clip upon a chain hung round his neck. "It is inscribed, *By God's will.*"

"You have great need of such a talisman?"

"We lead here very eventful and memorable lives. We set our eyes on many wondrous and wonderful sights deep down below the ocean's sun-scorched surface, and many strange and exotic sea creatures. Every deep dive shows the sea change and turn into something rich and remarkable—as the drowned man whose eyes turned into pearls and his bones into coral."

"You bear, I see, the mark of one of those sea perils." Yusuf pointed at the long reddish scar girding the length of Malik's ribs. "Will you tell me the tale which lies behind it?"

"Know, my son, that mine is a strange and terrible tale," Malik answered willingly. "And if it were engraved with a needle-graver on the corners of the eyes it would be a warning to whoever would be warned!"

"Say on, my sheik."

"Know that pearls can sometimes foretell tears, or even bring tears to their possessors."

"How so, my sheik?"

"Once a very long time ago," Malik recounted, "I went in search of the fabled black pearl of golden lights. I dove to a bank of coral lying in a sunken abyss some two-hundred fathoms deep. It was surrounded all around by a bed of boiling emeralds. The coral's jagged edges were sharp, and cutting, and made my blood flow from a hundred wounds. But I did not care. Its treasures of pearl were guarded by a gigantic sea-spider with blazing green eyes. I came to close quarters with the monster and did great battle with it. And now I bear the mark of its deadly embrace."

"Why would you risk such grave danger for so tiny a treasure?" Yusuf stopped sipping his coffee, looking agog.

"To win the favor of the woman I loved—and to whom I had pledged my heart and soul."

"What of this woman? What came to pass with her?"

"By Allah, I wish to let pass her story and think no more of it—at least for now."

"As you wish. What of us then?"

"It comes to my mind," Malik deliberated, "that you should serve my apprenticeship so that you may be master of a trade which will serve you. And if such be your desire this would be becoming to you."

"My deepest desire, my sheik," Yusuf mused, "is to find again my fatherland and serve it."

"By Allah, my son, you make me share in your desolation and despair!" Malik sympathized. "So do you desire to be with me as my apprentice? If so I will prepare you in the craft of pearl-diving, and be your fellow and companion in God's glory and gain. You will work and toil every day, and be my young man, and I will protect and preserve you."

"I will consent to that," Yusuf willingly relented.

"Then let me and you be in league together. Surely, my Yusuf, you are an able-bodied fellow, and when you will have toiled at this craft, you will be a most exemplary diver. And right now the best judgment is this: that we make haste then and do not delay in your instruction."

"I hear and obey."

"Now I must go on my way, my son." Malik handed Yusuf the softly smoldering dish of ritual incense he had inhaled from.

"My sheik, you never told me how you knew of me here." Yusuf took a whiff of the wafting smoke.

"It cannot be told by me," Malik counseled him. "Put your dependence upon God, for one other than myself must tell you. If it be the will of God—Whose name be exalted!—the affair is for God to decide, and what God wills is that which will be."

Together they stood up and Malik grasped Yusuf tightly at his shoulders, and Yusuf laid firm hold of Malik's arms as they penetrated each other's eyes.

"For now," Malik bid him a warm goodbye, "I pray Allah that He preserve you and prolong for me your life."

"And yours," Yusuf said. "It is well."

Then Malik retired to the tent and returned holding a big, spiraling conch shell which he pressed to his lips, gulping in a deep breath of air and sounding it like a bellowing but mournful horn. Then he handed the shell to Yusuf.

"Follow your good fortune," he saluted him.

"You are the superior in generosity to me," Yusuf praised him, looking perplexed returning his salute. "Godspeed. God grant we meet again."

Abruptly a great, gigantic and golden seahorse burst up out of the water at the edge of the nearby flowing stream, the spiked and peaked body armor drenched and dripping wet. Enormous fins on the giant creature's middle spine, on the sides of his swaying head and below his bloated stomach pulsated and beat wildly in the wind. As the mammoth body bobbed up and down in the streamlet, the snaky and serpentine coil of a tail curled up, turning and twisting tortuously in the water. Even more incredibly a jewel-studded saddle was laid upon the seahorse's back and bound by two girths strapped beneath his bulging breast. Yusuf stared agape as Malik abruptly leapt to the seahorse's back, slipping his feet into iron stirrups and laying firm hold of leather reins harnessed to a gem-encrusted collar.

"The night may be cool," Malik predicted. "Let my horse kindle your fire!"

With pressed knees he goaded the seahorse's flanks and, quite unexpectedly, the seahorse puffed out cheeks, blew open a long snout and—with a powerful poofing sound—spurt out a burst of fire which bolted to a pile of firewood, igniting it in a flash. Smiling satisfied, Malik put on his horn nose-clip and suddenly descended upon the seahorse's back and disappeared beneath a swirling wash of waves.

"There is no strength nor power but in God, the High, the Great!" Yusuf exclaimed, staring down with wonder at the splendid conch shell he was left holding in his hands. "Surely there is a profound mystery in this man!"

FOUR:
MONARCH OF FIRE

PILGRIMAGE

"As for the true believers, the Jews, the Sabaeans, the Christians, the Magians, and the pagans, Allah will judge them on the Day of Resurrection. He bears witness to all things."—Surah XXII, 17

MUKALLA, *Port City in the Land of the*
Red King, in Southern Arabia

L ooming resplendently at the very edge of the Arabian
Sea the great city of tall, whitewashed buildings lay
crowded and closely packed onto a narrow seaside
shelf washed by the calm, brilliant blue waters of a
small unsheltered harbor. A bright full moon shone in the dark
blue-black sky, throwing its beamy light upon the softly rippling
bay waters, glimmering with the burning lights reflected from
the tall latticed windows—glazed in deep turquoise blue—of
lofty, sky-climbing buildings. Towering minarets of several
grand mosques rose in scattered spots from among the high flat
rooftops. Soaring close behind the full length of this sea-skirt-
ing city were the deeply-tinged, precipitous cliffs of an ominously hovering reddish-brown mountain.

Standing majestically tall upon a small projecting prom-
ontory was the seaside royal palace with its splendid seacoast
views stretching at length on either side. Built of huge and hard
reddish sandstones—mortared with lime and roughly surfaced
with whitewashed stucco—its front marble stone wall was dis-
jointed by a series of deeply recessed and narrowly arched pilasters reaching from the ground to the sky-high cornice. Topping
off the palace was its magnificent upper kiosk—or belvedere—
with its many latticed windows, carved casements and skylights
mounted and edged with lustrous glazed tiles. Stretching even
farther before the palace to the very edge of the seashore, lapped
and splashed by gentle ocean waves and swept by the gusty cool
sea breeze, was the wide-open, marble-slabbed sea-terrace overlooking the city's quiet harbor.

A scepter of red gold capped by a forbidding bronze bull's
head swung easily at the side of the tall, slim man wearing the
long, flowing and loose-fitting white robe of gold-embroidered
brocade and strolling in long strides across the wide-open
promenade toward the sea-viewing stone balustrade. Standing

solidly at the balustered handrail was another man—tall and large—looking out at sea, his clenched fists buried deeply in his hips, his richly gold-embroidered robe and mantle of red silk flapping and flying in the air as the buffeting sea-breeze beat up and down his entire body.

Approaching the balustrade from the horseshoe-arched palace doorway behind the first man had features as dark as his closely-cut, jet-black beard and wore a deep black patch over his missing left eye. Crowning his head was a great crimson red muslin turban. He stepped right up to the other imposing man standing at the low-pillared balustrade, stopping near to the rear of his right shoulder. Standing at the balustrade the second man had a strong, powerful-looking carriage and manly bearing as he looked out intently and meditatively over the shimmering deep blue sea. His rough-cast profile showed he had dark, deeply-etched features and dark bushy eyebrows, furrowed from his being lost in deep contemplative thought. Upon his shiny bald head, matted around his ears with thick tufts of silver-gray hair, rested a great crown of red gold set with inlaid jacinths and jewels and capped at its crest with the familiar, forbidding bronzed bull's head. Prudently the white-robed man carrying the scepter addressed him.

"You sent for me, sire?" he asked.

"A sea of troubles lies before me, Bahram, in which I fear I am drowning," the regal-looking king answered solemnly, keeping his reflective eyes riveted without turning on the moonlit-bathed waters spreading far and wide before him.

"I read signs of trouble in your voice, my lord," the summoned liegeman sympathized before his voice grew markedly indignant. "What has provoked in you this melancholy? Tell me who among the emirs and sultans of the kingdom has become your enemy. Tell me who dares to defy you—or oppose you—that we may attack him and gouge out his very soul from between his sides!"

"My breast is shrunken and crumpled and I desire some distraction from it," the king said grimly.

"My lord," the liegeman suggested, "would you enter the palace garden and amuse yourself with the sight of the flowers and trees it contains, or look up at the planets and stars and marvel at the beauty of their configuration?"

"In truth my soul inclines to nothing of that kind," the king answered decisively.

"My lord, would you then go about the palace and amuse yourself with the sight of your many concubines asleep in their chambers?"

"My vizier, the palace is my own, and the female slaves are my property, yet my soul inclines to nothing of that kind."

"My lord, would you then have the sages, wise men, poets and men of learning come before you and recite verses or tell you wonderful tales and adventures?"

"My soul inclines to nothing of that kind," the king said, unflinching.

"My lord," the liegeman persisted, "would you then perhaps have the pages and cup companions come before you and entertain you with their whimsical wit and witticisms?"

"No, my vizier," the king himself grew distinctly indignant, "nor do I wish to hear the melancholy music of our court musicians. My soul inclines to nothing of that kind."

"My lord," the liegeman pleaded, "I would rather die right here and now than see you suffer this anxiety. Strike off my head then and perhaps that will put an end to your sadness and dispel the uneasiness which afflicts you."

At long last the king turned abruptly to his liegeman and glowered at him with his dark, deep-set eyes.

"Perhaps you tempt the Fates too far," he said gravely. Then pensively he looked once more out to sea, his voice sad and somber but gradually voicing bitter and wrathful anger. "No, my vizier, the enemy now besieging us threatens from without not from within. Do you forget that ours is the very last stronghold of our great Magian Empire, and that if our fortress falls our kingdom will be overrun by these Arab invaders who call themselves Muslims? Even now they slaughter and enslave our people. They pillage and plunder our holy cities and towns. They raze our fire temples and ravage our lands. We have become a nation of refugees and the only thing saving us from total extinction are the sheer numbers of our race. Do you forget how they beat and torture us for our faith and bribe us to convert to their perverted religion? Do you forget how they tax us and extort from us tribute to make us buy our protection from their death-dealing destruction? And they have the brazen audacity to call us pagan infidels!"

Abruptly the king slapped violently his left hand with his right.

"My King of the Age," the liegeman affirmed mindfully, "we have faced this perilous menace from the outside for a very long march of time. Surely something else distresses you and brings you to this sad state of mind. I am your Grand Vizier, and I do not know what it is. But you know I am like your son and your slave. You have both reared and mastered me. Who then beside me can know and stand in my place before you? Tell me then the cause of this melancholy, my king, and perhaps God will give you solace by my means."

"My faithful vizier," the kind said penitently, "I should not have distressed you as well. Leave me in my sadness and grief, for the sorrows in my heart are enough for me."

"My king," the vizier insisted deferentially, "the Hashimee vein of anger rises between your eyes. So I beg you to tell me the true cause of this grief and heartache before you resolve to dismiss me. What is it you desire? Have you not all that any man could ever wish for? Or do you desire an even greater and richer kingdom? Or is there some extraordinary treasure for which you have a longing?"

"No, my lord Bahram," the king's long face drooped from brooding upon his heavy sorrow. "You know very well that I am overwhelmed by wealth and power. My melancholy comes not because of riches, nor possessions, nor because of anything but this: that I have grown old and alone, and fallen ill, for I have been blessed with no male child—no son. I am destitute of a son. So when they finally bury me then will every last trace and vestige of me be obliterated, and my name will become extinct and outsiders will seize my throne and my kingdom, and no one will ever remember me. What will I do?"

Before he could answer the king turned to directly confront his vizier.

"This violent sickness has set upon me and perhaps it is that which will cause my death," he mused sullenly. "So I have summoned you to consult you about this affair, and desire that you give me the advice which you judge best, for I am in fear of my kingdom after me and have no son to follow me. And because of this I am left in a state of sadness and grief night and day."

"My king," the vizier commiserated, "you melt my heart but perhaps God will yet bring something to pass. So rely on the Almighty One and be constant in prayer, and beseech the Lord to grant you a son, for perhaps by such prayer you will gain your wish."

"For forty years now I have prayed, my Bahram," the king unhappily protested. "For forty years I have lived with my wife and have not been blessed by her with a son. I possess many concubines, but by none of them have I been blessed with the boon of a male child. I think of this and grieve that the greater part of my life has passed and I have not been granted a son to inherit my kingdom after me—as I inherited it from my fathers and forefathers. Because of this severe grief and violent vexation come to me."

"Be joyful, my king," the vizier objected deferentially. "I foresee for you long life and many years in your future from which to take the blessing of a strong son."

"I doubt the truth of these words, my venerable vizier," the king said with deep disbelief. "I am stricken in years and feel my bones are wasted. Even though I have a wife and many concubines—each of whom I am in the habit of lying with one night in turn—it still preys upon my mind and disturbs me that I have never been blessed with a son. In truth, I fear my kingdom will be lost when I die, for that I have no son to succeed me. I should at least like to have a son to whom I could one day leave my kingdom. Who will take my kingdom after my death? Will any but a stranger take it? I will be as though I had never been."

With a gesture of bitter disappointment and frustration the king threw up his hands as he moved slowly along the balustrade—his vizier warily following him—until he stopped once more, leaning restlessly upon the handrail.

"Everyone else is overjoyed from rejoicing in their children," he lamented resentfully. "Only I have no son, and tomorrow I could die and leave my kingdom and my throne and my lands and my treasures and my riches, and the outsiders would take them and no one would ever remember me. There would not remain any memory of me in the world."

"My king," his vizier reassured him, "your greatness is such that should you die tomorrow your fame and glory alone, which are legendary and world renowned, would preserve your memory to the end of time—even for want of a son."

Deeply preoccupied with his grief the king listened but heard nothing.

"My vizier," he pensively complained, "my heart is sunken, my patience is overcome and my strength is weakened because I have no son. This is not the usual way of kings who rule over lords and paupers, for they rejoice in leaving children and multiplying by them the number of their posterity. What then is your counsel, my vizier? Point out to me what is most advisable."

"For now," the vizier counseled, "I advise simply that you rest and pause to pray and take your ease, and find something good by which to amuse yourself and drive your dull care away—something by which to gladden your heart and raise your spirits."

"My vizier," the king said sorrowfully, "I am so severely agitated and heavyhearted this night that I desire of you whatever may raise my spirit and broaden my breast with amusement. So say on."

"My king," the vizier declared, "it has come to my knowledge that in your Pavilion of Pictures there appears something unveiled which will lighten your heart and make all care depart."

"Then do accompany me there," the king commanded.

"Hearing is obedience," the vizier bowed compliantly.

§

Through a horseshoe arch of red and white stones the king and his grand vizier entered and strolled into a long, high-ceilinged hallway leading into a grandiose gallery built of white marble walls encrusted with emeralds, rubies and other semi-precious stones. Multi-colored marbles formed geometric designs—lustrous eight-pointed stars and turquoise crosses—with complex carved and painted configurations adorning its ceilings. Stained glass windows were mounted in plaster. Farther along the great corridor walls were divided into sections made of alabaster, carnelian and jasper stonery and mosaic work. Interspersed along the way were little stone or stucco figures or figural bas-reliefs of royal personages, courtiers and warriors showing scenes of their adventures and exploits. After a time they came to a vaulted, hemispherical chamber—octagonal in shape—paneled in wooden lattice-work and buttressing a domed cupola. Its large arched doorway—its border richly ornamented and crowned with a streamered crescent—showed figures of lions, eagles and other fabulous birds. Elaborately carved floral scrolls decorated panels set upon either side of the arch.

Inside the far inner wall of the deep recess a tall and wide mosaic mural of lustrous glazed tiles stood out and stunned the beholder's senses with amazement. Pictured in the mosaic tableau was a most beautiful young woman wearing a shapely and slim-fitting bluish-black indigo dress embroidered with silver-metal thread. Red and green embroidery rounded her neckline and cuffs, and bars fringed her shoulders as silver bars did her waistline. Green, red, silver, yellow and metallic gold braid edged her costume's hemline.

Her face was as graceful as her dress was colorful—a perfect oval, brighter and more beautiful than the darkest night's fullest moon; golden and more radiant than the shining sky's most blazing sun. Shaping her face was a thick cascade of ebony black hair which hung heavily in rolling waves to her delicate shoulders. Her forehead was high and shiny. Her eyes were like deep bronzed almonds lined with jetty black kohl and set delicately beneath black, thinly arched brows. Her nose was straight and slender. Her blushed cheekbones were high, finely chiseled and carmine in color. Her smiling, pressed lips were full, lush—and to the awestruck eye—supremely soft.

For a long time lost in wonder the Red King gazed pensively at the beautiful female figure emblazoned in colorful mosaic tile-work.

"Her face is so alive and vital she almost speaks," he said finally.

Engrossed by the striking sight the king murmured to himself in awe and amazement.

"Surely none more beautiful than she has ever been seen on the face of the earth," he said, spellbound. "She captivates my reason and numbs my mind. My vizier, do you know who among women is the original model of this portrait that we may search for her?"

"No, my king, I do not know the model of this portrait." Bahram pointed to the foot of it. "Come, read this inscription."

Leisurely the Grand Vizier stepped up and stooped to reach out and smoothly pass his fingertips over a tiled panel showing geometric patterns with a simple scrolled border and bearing a

Persian inscription.

"*Jamila—the Princess Pearl of the Sea*," he read softly.

"My lord," he straightened himself and looked at the king with an air of urgency, "if the model of this portrait does exist—and if her name is Jamila and she does live in this world—I will make haste to look for her, without delay, so that you will gain your desire. I implore you then, my king, that you cast off this grieving."

"Would I ask the artist about the model of this picture—who she was or is—then perhaps he would tell me," the king looked back at his vizier, anxious and approving. "And if the model of this is living I might gain access to her. And if this is a picture portraying no particular woman I would have done with being enamored of it, and not torment myself because of a thing which does not truly exist. So fetch him here to me."

"I am here, my great lord king."

From a gray-bearded old man wearing a white turban and a short blue worker's smock pulled over petticoat trousers, bowing prostrate and kissing before the king the ground between his hands, came the whispered words. Then he clenched the skirt of the king's ankle-length red silk garment and kissed it as well.

"Peace be on you, my exalted and noble king!" he said into the ground without looking up.

"On you be peace, and the mercy of God, and His blessings!" the king saluted him. "Rise and face me."

Slowly the old man stood up, meekly biting the ends of his fingers and humbly waiting for the king to address him again.

"By God, you are an excellent artist!" the king commended him.

"You honor me beyond all measure, my kind and beneficent king!" the artist acknowledged in gratitude, glancing up only fleetingly. "I do take pride in cutting each piece of tile to its own most suitable shape."

"In truth you have done well," the king praised him. "You

are Muslim, are you not?"

"Yes, my lord," the artist answered reluctantly, bowing his head and fearing to look up at the commanding king.

"You have nothing to fear," the king reassured him, gently laying both his hands upon the old man's shoulders. "What is your name, my uncle?"

"Kaliq, my lord."

"Tell me, Kaliq, what draws a Muslim to the land of the Magians?"

"Only here in this kingdom am I free to practice my craft, my king."

"What do these words mean?"

"The followers of Islam believe that the maker of an image portraying anything of life will be commanded on the Day of Judgment to give it life," Kaliq explained, showing fully his deeply lined and leathery brown face, "and failing that will be duly sent to the Fire!"

"Yours is a forbidding faith," the king declared. "Tell me then, my uncle, something of a story and how you came to emblazon this picture."

"My king, will I tell you of a thing I have actually seen with my eyes, or a thing of which I have heard with my ears?"

"If you have seen anything extraordinary and worth the telling, tell me and let me hear that, for hearing a thing as told by others is nothing like seeing it."

"Hearing is obedience. My king, give up to me then your hearing and your reflection."

"My uncle, behold! I hear you with my ear, and see you with my eye, and take heed of your words with my mind."

"Once I was going about in a vessel upon the sea to fish," Kaliq recounted. "The wind cast me towards an island, and I looked and saw this most beautiful of women standing stark naked by the shore of the sea. But when I cast my eyes on her, I was somehow frightened to death of her and steered away my boat in flight. So she called out to me, making many signs to me, and declared herself to be a human being and not one of the Jinn as I had feared. She desired to embark in my vessel, but I sailed swiftly away and escaped. But never for the life of me will I forget the beauty of her face. And so I have pictured and preserved her here."

"This is a wonderful tale, my uncle," the king looked rapturously pleased. "You have cheered me with your company this night. Now you have my leave to go your way."

"On my head and eyes be it!" Kaliq bowed, saluted and shuffled off along the echoing gallery corridor.

"Bahram!" In the same breathless breath the king turned to command his Grand Vizier. "Accompany this artist and find out everything that is known and knowable of the Princess Jamila. I wish to remain and look upon her a while longer."

"Yes, my lord," Bahram smiled knowingly. "To hear is to obey."

Then he sauntered off to follow after the elder artist. Once more the Red King contemplated the magnificent mosaic portrait of the beautiful princess, Jamila, and mindfully mused.

FIVE:
PRINCESS OF THE SEA

THE MOON

"The Hour of Doom is drawing near, and the moon is cleft in two. Yet when they see a sign the unbelievers turn their backs and say: 'Ingenious magic!' They deny the truth and follow their own fancies. But in the end all issues shall be settled."—Surah LIV, 1-3

Over the Isle of Pearl's expansive but quiet lagoon the big full moon hung perilously low—a great, blazing white globe haloed in a hazy ring of luminous light, spreading its day-like brilliance in a vast swath across the softly shimmering waters washing up gently against the shore, looking like at any moment it would plummet and shatter the calm, glassy surface with a violent and tumultuous splash. It was the very same moon shining over the Land of the Red King an ocean's distance away.

Yusuf knelt upon a prayer-carpet spread near the entrance to his tent and read from the open holy book—the glorious Koran—held up from the floor by a small wooden stand. Outside the tent a blazing fire crackled noisily and threw its flickering, flame-colored light upon his sun-burnished features, expressing deep preoccupation with the sacred words he was so reflectively reading. Across his face another flashing blaze—quite different and distinct from that of his campfire—suddenly shed its light—resplendent and lapis lazuli in color. He looked up and saw that a spacious part of the calm cove waters were steeped and splattered with this light, shooting out luminescent beams in all directions across the watery surface from a central, radiating point. Warily he arose and walked toward the seashore—surprised and curious. With bubbles percolating at the spot where the shooting beams of blue-violet light converged at dead center the water boisterously boiled.

A startlingly strange and wondrous figure—mysteriously dark and lithe—began to gradually emerge from the bubbling, beaming waters. Slowly but surely it arose from the shallow depths until it abruptly stopped and stood ankle-deep in the shoreline surf—seawater rolling and dripping off its sleek and smooth body. Its form was tall, shapely and slate-gray—but distinctly and definitely female! It was comely, having the heavy hips and full bosom of a curvaceous woman. Only its skin looked more like some sea creature's slippery hide than human flesh, but was unwrinkled and without scales. So was it human or beast? Just as Yusuf caught sight of the figure's slender and slick face the luminous blue-violet light coursing and circulating its way through the placid ultramarine waters suddenly faded and dissolved, leaving the odd figure darkly silhouetted against the bright moonlight. Afraid, he stood aghast and started to move slowly back, retracing his steps through the sand and inching his way towards the tent.

"Come nearer to me, my brother," the dark figure suddenly spoke to him in a hauntingly beguiling but softly sensual voice. "Do not flee from me, for I am a human being like you."

"Who or what are you?" Yusuf asked, distrustful and disbelieving.

"How soon you have forgotten me!" the figure answered assertively. "I am she who worked a good deed for you and by God's aid delivered you from your enemy at sea."

Yusuf carried his thoughts back until the sight of the galley ship slave-driver raising his grappling iron to strike at him suddenly flashed across his memory. Then he slowly lifted up his eyes to look straight into the strange figure's own glinting, copper-colored eyes.

"You?"

"Yes."

"Then are you not of the Jinn?"

"Yes, but I am also a woman—a believer in God and His Disciple."

"There is no strength nor power but in God, the High, the Great! Who cast you into the sea?"

"I am of the children of the sea. We are a lesser known race of the Jinn called the Divers and Plungers of the Sea. We are a kingdom obedient to the commandments of God, and we are compassionate towards the creatures of God—whose name be exalted!"

"Have you a name?"

"Know, my brother, that I am Jamila—daughter of the sea. My mother was one of the queens of the sea and she died giving me birth. My father is the king of this domain and he lives in the Palace of Pearl."

"How do the people of the sea walk through the water without drowning to the core?"

"By the power of the names engraved upon the seal-ring of Suleyman—on whom be peace!—we walk through the sea with our eyes open just as you walk over the dry land."

"And no harm comes to you?" he looked incredulous.

"Know that we walk in the sea with our eyes open and we see all that is in it," she said. "We also see the sun and the moon and the stars of the sky as if these were on the face of the earth. And this brings us nothing of harm. Know also that there are many peoples in the sea and as many living creatures as live on the land. And all that lives on the land compared to all that lives in the sea is but a very small matter."

Yusuf stopped dead in his tracks, but when the forbidding figure drew near once more he moved away in retreat. She smiled and flashed her gleaming rows of chisel-shaped teeth.

"My brother," she reassured him, "no harm will come to you, for by Allah my eye has not been delighted by any but yourself. So praise be to God who has shown me your face!"

She moved slightly toward him again until she stood out of the tidewater's gentle reach upon dry land.

"My brother," she entreated him, "tell me then who you are and what brought you to this place."

"Surely my story is long," Yusuf said timidly, "and I fear that if I tell it to you the time which it will demand will be too long for us."

"It is not as I imagined of you, my Yusuf!" her voice uttered bitter disappointment. "Alas, for the ways of fate and lot!"

Languidly she turned to go back to the sea. Yusuf thought better of her departing and called out to her.

"My sister," he implored her, "graciously grant another look upon me and retrace your honored steps."

Already she had descended into the sea-green shallows but,

upon hearing Yusuf's plea, turned around and waded toward the shore, stopping when she was waist-deep in water.

"For your sake I return," she said.

"You already know who I am," Yusuf said, surprised.

"You were made known to me by Fatima—the Devotee. It was I who fed you upon the beach after the storm. And it was I who sent you Malik—the diver—to offer you solace in a strange land. So set your mind at ease, take heart and tell me what has come to you from first to last."

"I hear and obey."

Yusuf sat down upon the soft sand of the beach with his right knee raised to tell her his story.

§

"And this is my tale and my history," Yusuf said once he had finished. "What of yours? How did the Jinn come to be among the believers?"

"God created the Jinn two thousand years before He created even Adam—the very first man," she recounted. "And among the Jinn there were believers and infidels of every sect—even as there are among men. And God sent to the Jinn His disciples and messengers—even as He had sent them to mortal men."

"Disciples came to the Jinn even before the Prophet Mohammed came to mortal men?" Yusuf marveled at her words.

"Well before," she affirmed. "God sent seventy disciples to the Jinn of the world."

"Say on, my sister," he urged, spellbound.

"In ancient times," she recounted, "long before the creation of Adam, a race of the Jinn inhabited the earth and swarmed over the land, the sea, the plains and the mountains, and the favors of God were multiplied upon them. They had government and prophecy and religion and law. But they transgressed and offended God. They opposed their prophets and made evil and wickedness abound in the earth, upon which God—whose name be exalted!—sent against them an army of Angels, who took possession of the earth and drove away the Jinn to the outermost regions of the world's islands, and made many of them prisoners."

"And were your parents both of the Jinn?"

"No, my mother was a Jinnee of the sea and my father a man of the land. So in truth I share in the nature of both, for I was born of both the land and the sea."

"Then you have been caught between two worlds—as one forced to swim an eternity against the tide," Yusuf sympathized.

"Yes," she gently stroked the glassy surface with her fluke-tipped limbs, rippling the water which embraced her slender waist. "Do you believe in destiny?" she abruptly asked.

"In the changeable or the changeless?"

"In either."

"I believe in the free will of men," Yusuf declared. "That man should use his free will by the laws of God and by his own good conscience and judgment, and that man should pray to God to bless his endeavors, or implore the Prophet or the saints to intercede in his favor, but always rely upon God for the end result—whatever that might be. And that—to me—is destiny."

"Yours then is not a passive belief," Jamila—the sea-jinnee—remarked.

"I am not a passive person by nature," Yusuf confessed with a smile.

"But what if your will defies or opposes the will of God?"

"To resist the will of God is criminal," Yusuf allowed. "But only by following God's law while following his own conscience and best judgment can man know he has let God work His will through him. Only then can man attribute the fruit of his actions to fate and destiny—to God's will."

"Have we Muslims not learned that the decrees of God, that fate and destiny are utterly absolute and unchangeable, that at the very beginning of creation God predestined on the Preserved Tablet in heaven every event, every action—at the same time commanding and commending good while forbidding and condemning evil?"

"You speak truly, my sister," Yusuf affirmed. "Only God did not predestine the free will. Sometimes God inclines it to good and sometimes the Devil inclines it to evil. So if man did not have the power to act contrary to God's will—to resist or even repudiate what God has predestined—then man could never be held responsible for his actions."

"I do not understand the meaning of these words," the sea-jinnee's prominent forehead furrowed from her puzzlement.

"I believe God judges our actions good or evil by our intentions," Yusuf explained. "And if we put our faith in God and act as believers of God, good actions and intentions can only deepen our happiness. But if we doubt and distrust our faith in God and act as infidels, evil actions and intentions can only deepen our misery, for a man can be admitted into heaven only by the mercy of God because of his faith."

"You are unlike other Romans then, for the Book says that evil was their undoing because they denied the revelations of God, and spurned and made a mockery of them."

"I am unlike any other man," Yusuf contradicted her, "for no race of men is evil. Only the actions and intentions of men are evil. And only God can know the hearts and minds of men."

"Does not God predestine the actions of men?"

"His actions—to be sure—but not his intentions."

"Do you not believe that God also predestines our travels?"

"That is our Muslim belief, my sister. Why so?"

"Because I wonder whether your voyage here to this island was an act of God's own destiny."

"Would that be important to you?"

"Perhaps," she said sadly.

"Why do I read signs of sorrow in your voice?"

"Were I not in fear and dread of being of the disobedient,"

Jamila avowed, "I should have avoided you completely, heart and soul, and stayed away from you. But I willingly surrender to what God has decreed to come to me—and to us. And you—if you set me free—you will become my master and I will become your mistress. Will you then set me free with the desire of seeing the face of God—whose name be exalted!—and make a covenant with me, and become my companion? I will come to you every day to this place and you will come to me. What do you say then, my brother, to this proposal?"

"Set you free from what, my sister?"

"You will dislike what I have to tell you."

"Tell me."

"A seer's prediction has foretold how I will marry a man," she confided, "but it is undecided whether he will be a man of my own choosing, or even if he will be a man I choose to love, for whether we are of the same sign and earthly element and how one might affect the other is also unsettled."

"How can there be a covenant between a human and one of the Jinn?" Yusuf asked incredulously.

"Any among God's brothers and sisters who recite together the Fatiha—the opening of the Koran—can make their covenant together."

"But if you fear the prospect of God's decrees, can you not pray God to change certain of His decrees and grant you at the same time the greatest happiness and the least misery?"

"Yes, my brother, but I will feel far stronger in my plea if you will bow to pray with me."

"Why should you honor me as your prayer companion?"

"I am not sure I know," Jamila hung down her head. "All I am sure of is that I desire to make this covenant with you: that I will commit myself to you and become bound to you, and die loving you, and keep our covenant and see none but you, and you will see my fidelity and my freedom from falsehood and the virtue of my good will towards you if it is the will of God—whose name is exalted!"

Yusuf choked with a sudden sadness as he fought mightily to drive back the tears welling out forcibly from his tired eyes.

"You strike me dumb, my sister," he moaned.

"My handsome Yusuf," she smiled sullenly, "will you keep our covenant?"

"By Him who raised up the heaven and spread out the earth over the water," he thoughtfully formed his resolve, "yes, surely I will keep our covenant."

"Then let the Fatiha be recited in confirmation of the covenant between us."

Jamila—the Jinnee of the Sea—waded her way out of the water and together, facing each other with bowed heads, she and Yusuf knelt upon the sandy beach to recite the Fatiha—the opening chapter of the holy and glorious Koran:

> *In the Name of Allah, the Compassionate, the Merciful!*
> *Praise be to Allah, Lord of the Creation,*
> *The Compassionate, the Merciful*
> *King of Judgment Day!*
> *You alone we worship, and to You alone we pray for help.*
> *Guide us to the straight path*
> *The path of those whom You have favored,*
> *Not of those who have incurred Your wrath,*
> *Nor of those who have gone astray.*

"My brother," Jamila declared, "we have become companions in faith and there is no difference between us, for we are one. And our only witness is but God and His moon."

Once they finally lifted up their eyes they sat down upon the beach nearer to one another and Yusuf gazed skyward.

"It is a magnificent moon," he marveled with praise, "like the full moon of fourteen nights."

"Once the light of the moon was as bright as the sun's," Jamila mused. "And God commanded the Archangel Jibril to dim the moon by touching it with his wings. And the moon became soft, subdued and silvery. And now the moon smiles with the traces left by Jibril's wings."

Yusuf heard her soothing words but his mind wandered, moving the sea-jinnee to stare at him curiously.

"Why do you suddenly grow so silent and solemn, my Yusuf?" she asked him.

"Because," he answered, looking intently into her bronze-colored eyes, "I was thinking how terribly tragic and painful it must be to be compelled to marry one you do not truly love. And..."

"Yes?"

"I pray it will never be the fate of your soul to suffer such pain, for if it were, I feel my own heart would suffer unbearably."

"My Yusuf," she mournfully implored him, "would you gaze upon me?"

Yusuf looked aghast upon her and watched her face suddenly and wondrously transform, taking on the very appearance of her mosaic portrait as it was emblazoned in the Pavilion of Pictures in the Land of the Red King, for she truly was Jamila—the Princess Pearl of the Sea! Just as suddenly the perfect beauty of her face glowed as bright and as brilliant as the full moon in its most radiant light.

Utterly mystified Yusuf stared at Jamila with disbelief and bewilderment. Slowly, gently—he reached out his hand and softly fondled the flowing black hair embracing her delicate ear, touching then her lobe, and at his touch she willingly inclined her head and nestled her soft cheek into his warm hand. Soulfully her eyes—then her own deep almond brown, gazelle-like eyes—peered deeply into his.

"Kiss me, Yusuf," she invited him, parting her lips to draw his. "Kiss me now."

Hardly believing what was happening Yusuf inclined easily to her and softly joined his lips to hers, feeling at once an immense warmth and tenderness he had never before known. But once she clung tightly to his neck with both hands and drew him to her his feelings turned swiftly to a fiery fervor.

"Come against me!" she gasped breathlessly.

Together they fell down to the ground—joined closely in a feverishly firm and inseparable embrace. Gently Yusuf held and caressed her shapely breast, and what was before strong and sinewy hide was then soft and supple flesh—human flesh! Her firm nipple pushed itself between his groping fingers as her breast swelled and flushed with its rising warmth. Exploring, their mouths melted into one another, their tongues deeply entwining.

"God forgive me!" she gasped.

Abruptly but gently she pushed Yusuf's chest away from her breast, arose and plunged furiously—headlong—into the calm ultramarine shallows, disappearing into the depths by the very same luminescent blaze of beaming, blue-violet light from which she had appeared, leaving Yusuf spellbound and confounded. For a long time he stared at the exploded waters until the gently undulating ripples finally passed and the surface shimmered once more solely with the soft moonlight. He wondered whether he was dreaming or simply losing his reason.

SIX:
SORCERER OF EVIL

THE FLAME

"May the hands of Abu-Lahab perish! May he himself perish! Nothing shall his wealth and gains avail him. He shall be burnt in a flaming fire, and his wife, laden with faggots, shall have a rope of fibre round her neck!"—Surah, CXI, 1-5

Through a great arched portal the Red King stalked, his scarlet robes flying as he left the long vaulted hall behind and strode furiously across the open square courtyard at the rear of the palace, passing the central, spouting fountain and picking his way amongst the court's aromatic plants to his private chambers.

"Good evening, my husband," the dark, older, venal looking woman reclined upon the room's divan-sofa greeted him when he entered.

"I have seen no good this night," the king lamented bitterly, shrugging his cloak off his shoulders and casting it aside.

"What are these words?" she feigned concern. "What troubles you?"

At the edge of the silk-stuffed satin mattress the king came and sat alongside the reposing woman.

"I look at my face in the barber's glass and see that the white of my beard eclipses the black," he said sullenly, thumbing his peppered beard, "and I realize that old age is the advance guard of death."

"But my husband," she heartened him, "you are amongst the strongest and mightiest of monarchs. Come, take your supper."

She gestured to a nearby food-tray bearing golden dishes of roasted fowl and lamb at which the king looked down his nose with disdain.

"I will eat nothing," he shook his head.

"What is the reason for this behavior and what has grieved you so?"

"You are the cause of my grief," he said, looking mournful and morose.

"Me?" she asked, surprised, "but why?"

"When I held court this day," he recounted, "I saw that every one of the chief officers of the realm had a son, or two sons, or more, and most of their sons were sitting in the manner of their fathers, because of which I regretted to myself: in truth my wife

JOSEPH COVINO JR

made me swear that I would never take another wife besides her, even though she is barren. So I lament having no son."

"Do you not think I lament and mourn our want of a son just as deeply as you do?" her eyes looked searchingly into his.

"I do not know."

"When a man demands anything of his wife he presses her until he gains it. But if the wife demands anything of her husband he will not grant it to her."

"What is it that you want?"

"When you have sworn, I will tell you."

"I swear it to you by my head."

"Swear by your divorce from me."

"I swear to you by my divorce from you," the king's voice rose with exasperation. "Now what is it that you want?"

"My husband, for what reason is this grieving? What has happened to you? Tell me, and acquaint me with the real cause of this."

"You have born me no children," he beat his own breast with bitter disappointment. "You have born me no son. Is that not enough?"

"I am your wife and I have been your closest confidant," she persisted. "And if you do not tell me your affairs, and make me acquainted with your secret, who will you tell your secret and who will you make acquainted with it?"

Adamantly the king shook his head and gave her no answer.

"Rouse yourself, my husband!" she exhorted him. "I would rather kill myself than see you in this pitiable condition."

"My wife," the king hung down his head, looking downcast, "I was ashamed to tell you plainly, and to make known to you that which has happened to me."

"I beseech you, that you tell me what it is that has happened to you, and do not be ashamed, for I am your consort and your wife and your counselor in all things."

Looking suddenly resigned the king sedately raised his

bushy brow.

"Tonight," he recounted, "I saw a portrait of a damsel whose loveliness was wonderful. When I saw this portrait my reason flew from my head. I became insane with my love of it and longed to reach out and caress it."

"My lord," she looked aghast, "what has afflicted you, and what is this portrait of which you have become so enamored, and why did you not tell me sooner?"

"My wife," he said with downcast eyes, "I was ashamed at you, and I was unable to speak of this affair, nor could I acquaint anyone with anything of it. But now you know my state. See then how you will act to bring about my cure."

"What means could be used?" she asked dubiously. "Were she of the daughters of mankind, we would devise a scheme to gain access to her. The law allows the raising of a lesser wife or a concubine with the investment of royal insignia to the rank of a privileged wife. So arise right now, my lord, and purge yourself of this anguish and gloom which plagues your heart. I will bring you a hundred damsels of the daughters of kings, and you will have no need or want of another."

"No," his voice turned adamant. "I will not give her up, nor turn my back on her, nor will I look for any other than her."

"But what if she is of the daughters of the kings of the Jinn, over whom we have no power, and who are not even of our own species? Who is able to gain possession of her? How would this be done, my husband?"

"How ever it must be done," he sternly insisted.

"My lost one," she said feelingly, reaching for the nearby flagon and pouring from it wine into a gold-gilded goblet, "come and freshen your spirit by drinking some wine. It will help deepen your sleep."

From her silver, garnet-set finger-ring and into the wine flaked a puny, concealed capsule of powdered henbane as she passed her hand over the mouth of the goblet.

"Take this cup," she heartened him, pressing it to his lips,

105

"for it will delight you."

Covering her hand with his own the king drained the cup with a relieved sigh. Then she took the cup from him and put it down upon the nearby table-service.

"Has it pleased you?"

"My wife, never have I tasted anything more delicious than this wine."

"Good, my husband," she folded him in her arms. "Now come and take your ease."

Against her bosom the king nuzzled his cheek and soon fell asleep. Gently she rested his head upon an ostrich-down pillow and—quite startlingly—stuck the sharp, glinting point of a double-edged, horn-hilted dagger blade to the king's bare, exposed throat.

All the many brass chains, sequins and triangular pieces of mother-of-pearl shell embellishing the queen's red-embroidered, black satin dress clattered noisily as she sat erect and moved markedly away from the reposing king, speaking scornfully to him even though he could then hear nothing she said.

"He did not lie who dubbed you the bullheaded one, for you are the simplest of the simpletons!" she uttered contemptuously. "So sleep out the night, and never wake again, for by God, I loathe you, and I loathe your whole body, and my soul turns in disgust from cohabiting with you. And I do not see too soon the moment when God will snatch away your life!"

Her whole face deeply contorted with profound repugnance.

§

Towering columns, their corniced buttresses connected by portal arches with sculptured busts in full round, stretched along the sides of the long, empty corridor, supporting the lofty vault. Alone Kaliq knelt in this great, vastly vaulted hall, oblivious to its echoing stillness. Into his cloak he reached and from his fine cotton waist-belt pulled out a battered, timeworn book. Somehow he never heard the footsteps when Bahram, the Red King's Grand Vizier, came up to him quietly from behind.

"My sheik," Bahram demanded, "sell me this book."

"My lord," Kaliq pleaded, looking startled, "it is without price."

"What is this book, my sheik?"

"It is the Book of Hidden Treasures."

"Are you a treasure-seeker?"

"Yes, my lord—or rather I was until I sought the beauty of living things by other means."

"How do you mean?"

Hanging his head down Kaliq meekly arose.

"Just as I told our noble and exalted king, my lord," he explained, "it is forbidden in the lands of the Muslims to make images portraying anything of life under threat of the Fire. Here in the land of the Magians I have found the peace and freedom to practice my craft."

"Then why do you keep this book if you no longer go in search of hidden treasure?"

"Because it contains many pictures which serve as subjects for my artistry, my lord."

"Let me see," Bahram demanded, holding out his hand to take from the artist his beloved book.

"Where lies the greatest hidden treasure, my sheik?" the vizier asked curiously, weighing the book in both hands.

"There lies in a secluded place on a remote island an immense Hoard and Treasure," Kaliq gravely confided, "the like of which none of the kings in this world has ever kept hidden. But more, the marvelous object in this Enchanted Treasure is a wonderful Lamp which, whoever possesses it, cannot be surpassed by any man on Earth, whether exalted by rank or enriched by wealth. Nor can the mightiest monarch of the universe take the full abundance of this Lamp with its might of magical means. And this Hoard can be breached only by the presence of an unknown young man."

"Young man?" the vizier mused pensively, leafing open the book's tattered leather cover and fingering through its faded pages. "And what of this magic Lamp? Of a truth we have heard from those who went before us, that the God of the Muslims granted to no one the like of that which He granted to the worldly king, Suleyman, and that he in turn gained that which no one other gained: that he was accustomed to imprisoning the Jinn—the Affreets and the Marids and the Demons in bottles of brass, that he stopped these up with lead and sealed them shut with his signet-ring. And being incensed with these Devils, King Suleyman then cast the bottles confining the Jinn into the great and bounding sea."

"Yes, my lord," Kaliq affirmed. "As you say, the magic Lamp is in the form of a copper cucurbite stopped with lead and sealed with the signet-ring of Suleyman, the great king, who was in the habit of imprisoning the Jinn and casting them into the sea. And if the Jinni is released from the Lamp, he is compelled to do the bidding of whoever commands the Lamp."

"Surely your king Suleyman was given an almighty domain," the vizier said approvingly. "What do you know of the bottled Jinn?"

"Only that they are very cunning and powerful beings of flight," Kaliq confided further, "created by God of the smokeless fire. They were created both male and female, good and evil, Muslim and infidel. And they can be either horribly hideous or highly handsome. They eat, drink and propagate their own species just as human beings do. Sometimes they even intermingle with our own species, and when they do, their offspring share in the natures of both species. Their bodies are invisible to men, except when they appear and disappear at will in great, gigantic pillars of blue smoke. They can take any form they please and often assume the shape of serpents, scorpions, wolves and jackals. They are of the land, the sea and the air. And they inhabit all manner of places on Earth—like baths, wells, graveyards and ruins. And they can be controlled only by certain magical charms and incantations."

"And by what charms and incantations did your king Suleyman use to keep control of the Jinn?"

"King Suleyman kept absolute power of the Jinn by means of a most wonderful talisman which came down to him from heaven: his wondrous seal-ring upon which was engraved the most great name of God. And by uttering the most great name of God he could keep his power and control over them, and by them perform even the greatest of feats and miracles!"

"Of what feats and miracles do you speak?"

"He foretold the future and compelled the Jinn to build for him great temples. It is said that by the power of his marvelous ring he could even raise the dead!"

"I long to cast my eyes upon one of those brass bottles of the Jinn," Bahram resolved, "and I mean to become Lord of the Lamp."

"My vizier," Kaliq assured him, "it is in your power to do so without even stirring abroad, but only by the presence of an unknown young man, for only he will be able to triumph over the forces which guard and protect the Lamp."

"What are these forces?"

"These are not known," Kaliq revealed, "since no man has ever triumphed over them. And so the Lamp has been made safe and so preserved. But if you send to this young man, bidding him to fly from his place to the island of which I spoke, he will bring you from there as many of such cucurbites as you have a mind to. If you are minded to do so it will be up to you to devise a stratagem to gain possession and lordship over the Lamp."

"Yes, my sheik," Bahram declared. "I am minded to do so, without even stirring abroad. But what island is it which preserves and makes safe the Lamp?"

"A fabled island lying at the outermost edge of the world known as the Isle of Pearl, which this book describes as one of the fatherlands of the Ancients."

Kaliq reached to point out certain pages of the book but Bahram held it fast to his breast.

"And you know nothing of this mysterious young man who must be the means of anyone gaining the Lamp?"

"No, my lord, except that he could bear the name of one of the prophets God had sent to the Jinn before the birth of Adam—the very first man."

"And the name of this prophet?"

"Yusuf, my lord."

"Come, my Kaliq," Bahram smiled affectedly at the artist, gesturing to the way before them, "let us walk on a little."

From the high, arched hallway portal opening up outside they emerged together and leisurely strolled along a narrow, sloping footpath made of coarse, roughhewn blocks of fieldstone and brick rubble set in mortar and sealed with plaster. Before long the rising footpath inclined even more sharply upwards and the two slowly climbed the very foothills of the lofty, reddish-brown mountain hovering high behind the royal palace and solemnly overlooking the quiet portside bay. Farther and higher the two plodded deeper into the pitchy black of night with only the dimming glow of moonlight leading them along their shadowy way.

"My master, where are we going?" Kaliq bewailed the rigor of their walk. "We have left the palace far behind us and have come up to this barren highland and, if our path is yet long, I have no strength left for walking, for truly I am ready to fall from fatigue. There is no pavilion before us, so let us turn back and return to the palace."

"No, my servant," Bahram resolutely refused. "This is the right path. Nor is our way ended, for we are going to set our eyes upon one which has never had its like amongst those kings and all who have ever come to look upon it. So rally your resolve to walk."

Presently into view the object of their walk loomed ahead.

Two twin dome towers shot up precipitously out of the darkness above the sky-climbing rooftops of stately houses, bearing horns like those of a great bull, set against the bleak backdrop of the black mountain hovering ominously behind them. Each dome rested upon squinches, or small conical vaults, set over a vast square base formed by four massive piers joined by equal arches. Built of huge, coarse but carefully-chiseled brick-shaped stones the towers were thickly coated with plaster and white-washed with stucco.

Their faces whipped by a gusty warm sea-breeze, Bahram and Kaliq came to the end of the steeply ascending footpath and passed through one of the four large, evenly-arched portals piercing each side of the great stone square buttressing the two domes. Inside was yet another but slightly smaller concentric stone square—pierced by an even smaller, narrower and much lower double-entry portal—through which the two ducked their heads to enter. They stepped inside a low-ceilinged, barrel-vaulted passage which was partitioned by wooden latticework, beyond which lay the tower's inner chamber. In each corner of the square base interior a squinch—one of the small conical vaults—connected the cavernous domes to the upper walls. These same squinches, or vaults, turned the inside of the stone square into an octagon at its base and a parabola at its summit.

Immense was the building's interior. At the far wall soared a gigantic, towering stone statue of a lordly human being, having a Persian king's flowing beard and heading a great winged bull's body made of stupendously sculptured limbs. Beneath the massive marble pedestal upon which the statue rested, and running its full width, was a long bench-altar with a hollow carved into its center to hold fire. Pure, glazed gray tiles faced the spacious chamber walls. At the center of the room stood a tall, imposing, ebony-black, octagonal-shaped pillar-altar—on top of which rested a huge urn-like vessel bearing a blazing fire. Before this altar was a large pyre and funeral pile.

Bahram left Kaliq standing aghast and awestruck at the vast

chamber and went straight to the bench-altar to set down the book beside a gold metal, throne-shaped sanctuary lamp burning pure oil. Flitting shadows danced across the tile-faced walls as wafting, ember-sparked smoke rose from the crackling pillar-altar crucible, coursing its way up through small holes bored into the high-vaulted ceiling. Once more the grand vizier laid firm hold of the bull-headed scepter he carried, tucked beneath his armpit, turned and raised his hands and voice in godly praise.

"Behold!" he exclaimed. "The Fire Temple of the great god Mithra! This is the Inner Sanctum—the undefiled and unseen sanctuary of the sacred fire—the highest and most victorious king of fires—and my own noble namesake: the great Bahram!"

In front of himself he lunged forward his scepter.

"And this," he sang out, "is the Mace of Mithra—the symbol of the war I must wage against the forces of evil!"

Then he gestured to a small, round, black pillar of solid stone standing low by the taller, octagonal one.

"My Kaliq," he commanded, "sit yourself down and take your ease, and presently I will amuse you by showing you marvelous matters whose like in this world you never saw. And when you are rested, arise and then I will show you, my Kaliq, things beyond the very realm of reality."

Obediently Kaliq sat down upon the flat-topped stone stump.

"But first, my Kaliq," Bahram importuned him, "tell me what you know or what is known of the princess Jamila."

Kaliq fidgeted restlessly upon his stone seat.

"She is said to be a jinni of the sea," he answered nervously, "a daughter of the sea whose father is the king who reigns over the island kingdom of Pearl: King Freton."

"And she lives on this island?"

"Yes, or in the waters surrounding it."

Kaliq looked aghast at Bahram as the grand vizier simpered sardonically—his eyes glinting deviously.

"My servant," Bahram smirked, "I have a mind to initiate you into the Mysteries of Mithra. So do not defy me, for as a friend comes back to a friend, we come again and again to the sacred Fire, bringing with us the spark of our own inner Fire, which ever burns upon the purified altar of our hearts. Obey me, then, in everything I command you to do, and soon you will forget all this toil and trouble when you look upon the marvelous matters I am about to show you."

Again Bahram turned around to the bench-altar and came down to Kaliq holding a ladle in his hand.

"The sacred Fire may not be seen by unbelieving eyes," Bahram admonished him menacingly, "and unbelieving eyes may not be allowed to see the sacred rituals. So you must either become a believer or lose your eyes."

Kaliq looked fearfully confused as Bahram fingered some fire-ash from the ladle and rubbed it to the artist's forehead, smearing it onto his skin.

"Dust to dust," Bahram chanted. "The Fire—all brilliant, bright and radiant—has spread the sweet-smelling fragrance of sandalwood and frankincense all around—but is at long last burned to dust. So is it destined for you. Like this Fire, may you do your best to spread—before your death—the fragrance of beneficence and the light of rightness!"

Again Bahram returned to the bench-altar and again returned to Kaliq, bearing a shallow metal bowl, holding it up in offering to the monstrous, human-headed winged bull-statue.

"With libations we will worship the all-powerful god— mighty Mithra—mightiest of the world of living beings!" he chanted. "We will pay homage to him with praise and reverence. With libations we will loudly worship him!"

Invitingly he held out the bowl to Kaliq.

"Drink of this rejuvenating, life-giving cup of immortality," Bahram commanded him.

Reluctantly Kaliq took the bowl and looked askance, turning up his nose at the foul-smelling, yellowish liquid it contained."

"Drink," Bahram urged him.

Hesitantly Kaliq sipped from the bowl, dribbling the liquid from his lips, abruptly spitting out the rest from his mouth with utter disgust. Just as abruptly Bahram whacked Kaliq—quite insultingly—upon the back of his neck with the nine-knotted palm-stick he tucked under his armpit. By the blow the bowl and its liquid were sent flying and splashing across the floor.

"Fool!" Bahram bellowed. "I told you to drink!"

"My master, what have I done that deserves from you such a blow as this, for what is this drink which tastes so bitter and ill-flavored!"

"It is the consecrated water of the living bull!" Bahram cried.

Looking sadly sickened and repulsed Kaliq arose from his stone stump, but Bahram forcefully pointed his stick at him.

"Stay yourself there and keep yourself seated!" he roared ragefully.

Slowly Kaliq sat back down—intensely frightened and afraid.

With fear and trembling Kaliq watched while Bahram returned once more to the bench-altar before returning to him—holding in his hands the Mace of Mithra.

"And now," Bahram fatefully addressed Kaliq, "the Fire demands a blood sacrifice, and we must not fail to please and delight the Fire, for without sacrifice the world would be no more, and through sacrifice we are purified."

Before Kaliq Bahram stood, raising again his mace and his voice to the colossal, octagonal pillar-altar buttressing the blazing fire-urn.

"But purification can come only through the Fire which destroys darkness and evil," he chanted clamorously, "for the Fire is at once the destroyer and the preserver. All actions and deeds come out of the Fire, and the flame that burns heavenward reminds man of his final fate and destiny. The Fire is then the final conquest of brightness over darkness, of evil by good, for the Fire is truly the final equalizer—the final judge and avenger!"

Then he turned again to invoke the colossal bull-statue.

"Great god Mithra, Lord of Light, Lord of Countries!" he chanted. "You are the strongest of the strong, the sturdiest of the sturdy, the all-powerful, all-knowing and undeceivable one. You put people in their proper places. You smash the heads of the deceivers and falsifiers!"

Fearfully Kaliq flinched, but before he could fully react Bahram swung his mace at him, battering its bronzed bull's head violently against his, knocking him headlong off the stone stump and onto the hard stone floor.

Sluggishly Kaliq crawled prostrate across the stone floor, heaving, his head bloodied by Bahram's bull-headed mace—itself smudged with blood. Weakly he held up a pleading hand and looked up at Bahram with desperately imploring and terrorized eyes.

"Spare me, master," he begged pitiably.

"I have spared you," Bahram scoffed scurrilously, "to become the supreme sacrificial offering—to become the flaming fat of the Fire!"

Kaliq shook his head in silent, supplicating protest.

"I long to become Lord of the Lamp of Suleyman!" Bahram raved, grinning maliciously. "So my very first course of action must be to wipe out all outside knowledge of this affair—beginning, I hardly regret, with your own destruction, my knowing and knowledgeable sheik!"

Then he firmly grasped the bull's head, twisted and wrenched it, pulling from the hollow sheath of the mace's staff a long, narrow, gleaming, double-edged blade.

"And as you must wish to die like a Muslim," he said sadistically, "I will gladly and happily slaughter you like a Muslim!"

Then Bahram forcefully fell upon Kaliq, tightly clutched his hair, violently yanked back his head to lay bare his exposed throat—and lustily slashed with his deadly blade!

§

Warily the wife of the Red King entered the fire temple's inner sanctum and found Bahram—the Grand Vizier—excitedly stoking with a torch the blazing pyre and funeral pile upon which lay Kaliq's supine dead body. She drew near, bewildered, watching all the while as Bahram laughed loudly and madly like one possessed of a devil.

"At what do you laugh with such loud laughter as this?" she blurted out, dumbfounded by the sight.

Bahram whirled around to leer at her like one who had lost his wits.

"I laugh at a secret something which I have seen and heard but cannot tell!" he ranted.

"By force of necessity you must tell it to me, and tell me the cause of your laughter," she insisted.

"I cannot tell you."

"By our great god, what pretense is this?" she railed threateningly at him. "You laugh at no one but me, and now you would keep something from me. But by the Lord of the Fire! If you do not tell me the cause I will no longer keep company with you. I will leave you at once."

"What means this prying?" he scolded her. "Fear our god, leave these words and ask me no more questions."

"You must tell me the cause of that laugh," she persisted.

"Under pain of death I will not tell my secret to you," he refused.

Then he went to the wall to return the torch to its decorative sconce.

"No matter," the queen complained callously, "tell me your secret and die this very instant if you are so minded."

"Upon me there hangs a very strange tale," Bahram caustically confronted her once more, "but it is such that I can tell it to no one."

"I will not turn from it until you tell me, even though you come by your death," the obstinate queen stubbornly persevered.

"Very well," Bahram looked abruptly resigned. "Come closer that I may tell you the secret while no one sees or hears us."

As she stepped up to him he abruptly backhanded her face hard with his open hand, her whole head and body reeling from the blow, making her stagger and sink to her knees. She cried out loud, palmed her pained face with both hands and Bahram bent to violently grab her by her arms and wrench her to her feet.

"Now, will you ever again be asking me questions about what does not concern you?" he wrathfully challenged her.

Ruefully she hung down and shook her head.

"I am of the penitent!" she pledged. "By our god, I will ask you no more questions, and I repent truly and unerringly."

Gently Bahram lifted her chin with his finger.

"And what cause had you to stay away all this time?" he asked her feelingly. "I have not been content to drink even wine because of your absence."

"My lord, my heart's love and coolness of my eyes," she answered with tears in her eyes, "do you not know that I am married to the Red King, whose very sight I despise enough to despise myself when I am in his company? And did I not fear for your own sake, I would not let a single sun arise before smashing his city into a ruined heap of rubble in which the raven would croak and the jackal would prowl."

"You lie, damn you!" Bahram roared angrily. "Now I swear an oath by the valor and honor of men—which is excellent and noble—that from this day on, should you stay away until this hour, I will not keep company with you, nor will I join my body with your body. Do you play fast and loose with me—you cracked pot!—that I may indulge your sordid lusts—you vilest of sluts!"

"My beloved, and very fruit of my heart," she said soothingly, "there is no one left to gladden me but your dear and precious self. And if you cast me off, who will take me in, my beloved, and light of my eyes?"

"Why, your beloved husband of course: King Zahhak," Bahram sneered sarcastically. "And how is he this night?"

"Now he sleeps," she brazenly boasted. "I drugged his wine to make him sleep. Now he acts like some lovesick fool, for he drivels like a child about falling in love with the portrait of some eye-filling female."

"Yes, so I have seen and heard," Bahram affirmed, chortling wickedly. "And it will be through the means of this female that I will subvert and overthrow this impotent and ineffectual king—before he brings to our last land total wrack and ruin."

Intently the queen watched the vizier restlessly go the round of the imposing pillar-altar, reverently caressing its smooth ebony surface.

"I dream of a day when the breath of the great god Mithra will sweep again through his temples," he spouted, "fanning the ashes upon the altars of those ancient flames, and every altar will flash into fire, and again from heaven the answering flames will fall, making the Magian cult once more what it should be: a beacon light to the souls of men—the greatest cult of the world!"

Languidly Bahram lifted up his eyes to the blazing fire-urn set atop the high pillar-altar.

"As Fire," he intoned, "you are the delight of Mithra, and you must burn eternally, for time without end."

Then he turned again to the royal wife—the queen of the Land of the Red King—gently and warmly taking her face into his hands.

"And as fire you are my delight," he told her fervently, "and you too must burn eternally—for me."

Breathlessly and gluttonously he smothered her mouth with his own, letting his groping hands fall and run down over her heaving breasts.

"Now lie down and lift up your dress," he commanded her.

SEVEN:
GROTTO OF
LONELINESS

JOSEPH

"Joseph said to his father: 'Father, I dreamt that eleven stars and the sun and the moon were prostrating themselves before me.'"—Surah XII, 4

JOSEPH COVINO JR

"**A**h!"

King Freton awoke with a violent start, vaulting from his silk-stuffed satin mattress like one leaping from his skin—breathless, feverish, flushed with fear and trembling, his skin awash with beading cold sweat. His velvet-covered ostrich down cushion was soaked with wetness. Stripping off the silk coverlet from his drenched frame he sat up upon the edge of his alabaster couch, richly set with fine pearls, jewels and bars of red gold. Arising he took from a large cane-work chair the stiff, black-paneled woolen cloak which was draped over it. He put on the over-garment and pulled it down over him, straightening its folds and seams trimmed with silk cord and embroidered with silk floss.

"Muti!" he called out.

From an adjoining closet chamber a manservant presently appeared, bowing in salute.

"Yes, my lord, how may I serve?"

"Sound the beckoning horn," the king commanded.

Before long the king heard the mournful moan of a conch shell-horn blaring resonantly. Then he strode out of his private chambers and into the blazing, bright light of day. Passing through the pointed, keel-shaped arch of his apartment he set foot onto the raised flagstone platform hedging round the outer edge of the open courtyard outside—its border emblazoned with inlaid black and white marble and pieces of fine red tile. Only instead of reflective flooring the spacious center of the vast courtyard glittered with deep and resplendent spring waters. There was no central fountain or plant-decorated pavement but only voluminous spring waters. At the foot of an octagonal and arcade-enclosed courtyard surrounding that great deep water spring the king's chambers stood tall.

Stepping off his carpeted patio the king sauntered along the darkened arches of tunnel vaults set high upon massive round piers. Soon he came to a curtained portal flanked by two burly black slaves wielding glinting scimitars. One of the guards held the curtain aside as the king passed unprevented through the entry.

Echoing throughout the cool and damp passage the king entered could be heard the monotonous sound of persistently dripping water. It was a dark, low, narrow and roughhewn tunnel bored ruggedly through the limestone rock—its carved circumference remarkably even and uniform in shape. Taking a burning torch from a wall sconce at the tunnel entry the king set off along the darkened passage—the torch's flickering flame illuminating the way, glistening and stretching somberly before him. Turning and twisting, the rough rock tunnel wound sharply downward as the king descended deeper into the yawning bowels of the earth. At length the passage leveled and ran narrowly along a taller tunnel—walled in all around by a solid but translucent emerald-colored drapery of mineral-tinted rock. Finally the king came to his destination: a cavernous subterranean grotto.

Glistening, bulbous stalactites overarched the low ceiling of the small, cramped chamber closing in the lucid green pool of luminescent water. Upon another sconce affixed to the cavern wall the king hung his torch. Then he tread to the edge of the gently sloping strand of sandy beach fringing the placid pool— and waited.

Brilliant beams of scintillant lapis lazuli light abruptly shot and suffused their way throughout the water as bubbles percolated boisterously upward. Soon a dim and shadowy figure appeared beneath the serene surface of the pool, taking shape as a hazy blur and then as a darkish human form which rose gradually from the depths until finally bursting out of the water. Emerging from the pool came the merwoman—Jamila—jinni of the sea. Out of the pool she climbed—water dripping from her grayish, lithe and sinewy limbs—and stepped up onto the slender strand of beach. King Freton reached out and laid firm hold on both her outstretched hands, pulling her to her feet.

"Welcome and good cheer to you, my daughter," he greeted

her.

He caressed her cheek with his free hand as she awkward-ly but affectionately took his right hand into her fluke-tipped hands, kissing his sleeve in salute and lifting up her copper-col-ored eyes to meet his.

"And to you, father," she said reverently. "You called for me?"

"Yes, my daughter. Come."

He led her by the hand to a nearby fissured niche in the rock where set against the cavern wall was a couch of Indian rattan with ivory feet.

"Sit yourself down next to me," he said softly.

Together they sat down upon the couch—the king holding tight to his daughter's hands upon his lap.

"Did I ever tell you the legend of the Island of the Bereaved Mother?" he asked her.

"No father," she answered. "Would you tell me?"

"In ancient times," the king recounted, "a jinni sojourned on this secluded island and she—like you—was of the Jinn of the Sea. She loved a mortal man very deeply and became passion-ately attached to him. Only she was in fear of her unearthly family. Her desire having become excessive she went in search over the earth for a place in which to hide him from them. She found this island to be cut off from both mankind and from the Jinn so that no one of either of these races—except herself—could ever find their way to it. Then she carried off her beloved and put him there, and used to go to her family openly but went to him secretly. And so she kept on doing for a very long time until she bore him—on that island—a child: a daughter. And those mariners and seafarers who passed by this island on their voyages over the sea used to hear the weeping of the infant—like the weeping of a woman bereaved of her child, for she could never settle and live permanently with her child, by reason of which it is said there lives there a bereaved mother."

"Why do you tell me this story, my father?" Jamila asked.

"Because," the king answered solemnly, "I was the man, the jinni was your mother and the child was you."

"But I already know of my mother and of her deep love for you," Jamila looked perplexed. "You told me of this long ago because she had died giving me birth. I have even visited her undersea domain and often I have kept company with the sea-living people of her underwater kingdom. So why do you retell her tale in the manner of a legend?"

"My daughter," the king said gravely, "know that I have seen this past night a vision—a dreadful dream—as fantastic as any legend, and I fear for you because of it, and I fear there will come to you lingering anguish and anxiety."

"Why, my father? What did you see in your dream?"

For a moment the king mused to remember.

"I saw a great rock-bound coast," he recounted, unfolding his tale, "and a bloodthirsty band of highwaymen that abducted you and spirited you away upon their horses. They bundled you into a camel skin and there was some sort of seaside battle fought among hostile men. But then—lo and behold—a great and grotesque bird pounced upon you from the sky, snatched you up in its talons and flew away with you. So great grief and sorrow came upon me and I was touched with such exceeding terror and fear—which roused me from my slumber—that I awoke oppressed with melancholy and sick at heart, lamenting your loss."

"But whatever does your dream mean?"

"When I awoke with such dread and fear I summoned the interpreters and expounders and told them my dream. And they told me I would lose my dearest and most precious child, that you would be forcibly snatched up from me without your consent or mine. Now my daughter—my dearest and most precious one—you are about to journey to some unknown destination and I do not know what will come out of it to you. So if you are minded to journey somewhere do not go. But return instead to the sea and remain there."

For a moment Jamila hung down her head and then raised it again.

"My father," she assured him, "I can go nowhere. I must remain with you. Besides, who can invade our country or gain access to our Isle of Pearl, or your Castle of Crystal? If any invader landed upon it he would drown in a sea of destruction. So let your spirit rejoice in our condition, for no one has the power to trample upon our land without our consent."

"You speak truly, my daughter," the king affirmed. "But the Prophet has said that dreams are the only kind of divination worthy of belief. Good dreams, he said, are one of the parts of prophecy and nothing else of prophecy remains, for good dreams are from God, and bad dreams are from the Devil—and we must heed both."

"Then this story must be the fruit of devilish dreams," Jamila divined.

"I fear not, my darling one."

"Why so, my father?"

"Because," the king answered somberly, "the sight in a dream of anything black is inauspicious and of bad omen. And the monstrous bird I saw in my dream was the black ill omen of separation: the raven!"

"What will we do then, my father?"

"When any one of us has a bad dream," the king related, "the Prophet told us we should spit three times over our left shoulder, and seek our protection with God from the Devil three times, turning from the side upon which the dream was to the other."

"You will, I beg you father," Jamila smiled mirthfully, "give me your leave to go before you begin to seek God's protection."

§

A high, stately arch crowned the central entrance leading into the Red King's vast barrel-vaulted court and audience hall.

Upon the face of that royal arch two winged figures bearing crowns skirted the central royal crescent displaying a diadem. About that arch the fringe ended in a fluttering ribbon. Massive pilasters flanking the arch composed a sumptuous cosmological tree—a floral pattern of palmettes, palm leaves, pomegranates and undulating vines. Overarching the hall were several spherical domes and cupolas of varying sizes—their round bases resting upon semicircular arches projecting across the angles of the hall's smaller conical vaults or squinches. A spacious square the hall itself was vaulted with a high dome resting upon massy pillars. Arched entrances opened up in the middle of each face and column connected by buttressed arches and cornices, ranging along the walls bolstering the great vault.

Overspreading the whitewashed stucco walls and barrel vaults were fresco and mural paintings portraying royal battles, hunting scenes and excursions. Floors and walls were emblazoned with large, lustrous mosaics and marbles, richly and variously colored, forming luster-embellished eight-pointed stars and dark turquoise crosses. Interlacing, overlapping fretwork enriched wall panels with beaded circles and carefully molded frames. Overlaying the immense expanse spreading before the royal throne was a colored carpet spun in silk, gold, silver and encrusted with thousands of precious stones. Ivory and teakwood made up the enormous royal throne with its plaque and balustrades of gold and silver. Its stairs were gold-framed seats of black ebony and wood. A gold and lapis lazuli baldachin surmounted the throne, depicting the sky, stars, signs of the zodiac and the seven climates along with kings in their varying attitudes—banqueting, battling or hunting. Brocade carpets trimmed in gold and studded with gems and jewels completely draped the throne itself. Suspended above the throne from golden chains was a huge gilded crown which just touched the king's head whenever he ascended the throne to wear the crown.

Just then the crown King Zahhak held in his hands was a gilded ram's head adorned with emblems and precious stones.

Pensively he fingered the two rows of precious pearls adorning the crown's fastening diadem ending in two floating ribbon tails. Hemming in the great hall was a very high, heavy and richly woven gold-embroidered curtain. Silent and alone the Red King stood at the foot of his throne looking up at the huge, overhanging crown when his grand vizier, Bahram, passed through the curtain, crossed the vast stretch of carpet and softly stepped up to him.

"You summoned me to a private audience, my king?" Bahram reluctantly asked.

Disrupting his deep reflection the king solemnly turned to confront him.

"Yes, my vizier," he answered sullenly.

"May no harm come to you, my lord!" Bahram exclaimed. "Why do I see you change color and in pain? Tell me of your condition and what has come to you to change your color."

"I have much need to know more about the Princess Jamila, born of the sea, for surely she has enthralled me and ravished my reason. My vizier, whose daughter is this damsel and what has come of Kaliq—the artist who knows of her?"

Bahram looked loath to answer the king.

"My lord," he said grudgingly, "you know that one of the most meritorious acts a Magian can perform is to make sacrifice to Mithra."

Suddenly the king looked startled and distressed.

"Yes?" he asked expectantly.

"Kaliq has been taken to the fire, my lord," Bahram recounted coldly, "as a sacrifice offered with devotion."

Looking pained and displeased the king heaved a grim-faced sigh.

"What of his knowledge of the Princess Jamila?" he asked indignantly. "Did you cremate it along with him?"

"No, my lord," Bahram threw up his hands in a plea for indulgence. "Know, my king, that it has been told to me that the Princess Jamila is the daughter of King Freton—the sovereign crowned head of the Isle of Pearl."

Speechless and impatient King Zahhak rose restlessly to his throne, plunked himself down onto it, slapped down his crown onto his lap and stared down irately at Bahram.

"Well, go on," he ordered.

"She is of astounding beauty which words cannot describe," Bahram related, "and whose equal does not exist in this age, for she is endowed with the most perfect beauty and form. And it is said that when she approaches and draws near she seduces, and that when she turns away and recedes she kills, ravishing the heart and the eye."

Fidgeting in his throne the king looked only dubiously appeased.

"Then I will demand as my wife the daughter of this island king," he wrathfully resolved, "for I have seen by her portrait that she is, truly, endowed with the most perfect beauty and surpassing form. And I will give as her dowry a thousand pieces of gold. If her father consents my wish is gained. And if he does not consent I will take her by force in spite of him."

"Surely the great god Mithra keeps back harm and death from anyone who is true to him," Bahram heartened the king, inciting his resolve. "Neither the wound of the well-sharpened spear nor that of the well-darted arrow harms him whom Mithra comes to help. And the kingdom from which insult is hurled at Mithra is leveled to the ground. Only..."

"Yes, my lord Bahram?" the king asked anxiously.

"By custom we must also pledge to the bride's father a dowry of three thousand silver coins," Bahram reminded him.

"I will pay any price, my vizier," the king insisted with a dismissive wave of his hand, "for I long for not any but her. And I must have her or I will take to the sea and drown myself because of her."

Then Bahram's hands spread wide with suggestion.

"Could you not long just as well for a female slave unsurpassed in beauty and form by any in her age—one of perfect beauty and exquisite form, and endowed with all admirable qualities?"

"No, my vizier," the king answered adamantly. "Only the Princess Jamila can satisfy my need, which is great."

"My lord, I know your need," Bahram gently dissented, "but the Princess Jamila's father is a sovereign king, and his country is far off and away from us."

Shaking his head the king waved his hand disapprovingly.

"This makes no difference," he persisted.

"Give up this notion and go to your palace, my lord," Bahram rashly advised, "for in it are many female slaves like so many moons, and whoever of them pleases you do you take her. Or if none of them pleases you we will demand in marriage for you one of the daughters of the kings, more lovely and beautiful than even the Princess Jamila."

Then the king looked even more morose.

"Know, my vizier," he imparted, "that if the king buys a female slave whose rank and lineage are unknown he will not be aware of her ignoble ancestry that he may avoid her, or the nobility of her pedigree that he may make her his companion and mate. So if he does this she may perhaps bear him a son who may be a hypocrite and a liar, a tyrant, or a butcher and assassin! And she herself may be like the watery waste—the yield of which is barren and fallow—and then gain no nobleness or worth. Her child may be odious to the great displeasure of his lord, doing nothing he calls upon him to do, nor abstaining from that which he forbids him to do. So I will never be the means of such an affair by buying a female slave."

"What will we do then, my lord?"

"I desire instead that you demand in marriage for me one of the daughters of kings, whose rank and lineage are known, and whose loveliness and beauty are celebrated. If, then, you will point out to me one of excellent birth among the daughters of kings I will demand her as my wife and marry her, that she may bear me a son."

"Surely in truth your desire will be done."

"How so?"

"Have patience with me, my lord, that I may send to some king and demand of him her daughter in marriage and perform for you your wish. If she pleases you I will speak to him that he unite you to her in marriage. And if he does not give his consent we will tumble his kingdom around him, and send against him an army of which the rear guard will be with me when the advance guard is with him!"

"Do so, my vizier," the king approved, "and as I live and breathe I will grant you whatever you need, and I will give the king whatever he will demand for her dowry. And we will become fellow countrymen and kinsmen."

"I hear and obey," Bahram bowed slightly with his right hand on his breast, sensing he was dismissed.

"Carry on then this affair by your knowledge and wisdom," the king admonished him, "and go first to the Isle of Pearl and demand in marriage the daughter of their king, Freton!"

Bahram staidly submitted.

"Your desire will be done, my lord, but this will be difficult for you."

"How so?"

"For want of a son—a male successor to your royal personage—your royal wife, Anouba, could aspire after your throne and set her own eyes upon it," Bahram solemnly warned him.

"My wife? What are the meaning of these words?" the king asked, conspicuously concerned.

"Your wife holds the supreme position in your harem and is your chief consort," Bahram clarified. "She is your lawful wife whose children are the true successors to your throne."

"But you know full well that we have no children," the king objected.

"You speak truly," Bahram affirmed. "If your wife is barren the law allows that you may take a second wife to assure a son—a male successor to your throne. So in due time another wife or a concubine of a lower position could be elevated with the royal investment to the rank of a privileged wife. And by you she could bear your children."

"Then I must find another lawful reason to marry outside my kingdom," the king concluded.

"You may take to wife the daughter of the king of an alien people to bind the brotherly ties joining our domain to another," Bahram proposed.

"One such as the Muslim domain which even now surrounds and suffocates us like a creeping scourge?"

"Precisely."

"And what of religious dissent?" the king asked cautiously.

"Marrying outside our faith is frowned upon," Bahram conceded, "but it is not unthinkable."

Rising and setting down his crown upon his seat King Zahhak descended his throne and drew near to Bahram, grasping his vizier firmly at his shoulders.

"My Bahram," he confided, "you are my high priest, vizier and first minister. I pin all my hopes upon your great knowledge and wisdom, and I can do nothing in this urgent affair without your sage advice and counsel."

"My king," Bahram showed a mannered smile, "it is my opinion, then, that you send to the Princess Jamila's father an astute and discerning emissary, experienced and knowledgeable in the current of events in the world, that he may courteously and with good grace ask her in marriage for you of her father, for she has no equal in the distant and remote parts of the earth, nor in the near and near at hand, so you will rejoice and delight in her sublime face and form."

"Know, my vizier," the king nodded his accord with a knowing smile, "that none will go on this delicate mission but you, because of your consummate courtesy, good manners and civil tongue."

EIGHT:
GROTTO OF TEARS

THE EMISSARIES

"By the gales, sent forth in swift succession; by the raging tempests and the rain-spreading winds; by your Lord's revelations, discerning good from evil and admonishing by plea and warning: that which you have been promised shall be fulfilled!"—Surah LXXVII, 1-7

"**D**o you take warning!" Bahram threatened. "If your kingdom turns a deaf ear to our plea, my king will have no choice but to compel your king to meet his demand—by force of arms if necessary—even if my king must hold your king at sword's point!"

"In my king's name," Faris, Grand Vizier of the Isle of Pearl, cautioned him, "we will pardon your contempt of us and your want of courtesy and good manners, for you do not know us. But I would have you know that you will soon stand in the presence of our exalted king. Take heed, then, to speak softly before him and hold your uncivil tongue."

Conversing together the two grand viziers strolled along the rampart wall-walk running along the parapet—high atop the rubble, Romanesque wall projecting from the mouth of the mammoth cave gaping in the face of the sheer limestone cliff. Bahram stopped, resting a palm upon one of the solid merlons of the crenellated gallery and veranda overhanging the rock-bound coast far off below, and through the wall embrasure sedately looked out over the deep water ocean stretching far and wide before them. He barely blinked at the other vizier's admonishment and raised his eyebrows, smiling imperiously.

"If your king becomes satisfied with us and accepts our gifts," he affirmed without turning to face Faris, "and suffers us to make our overture to him, we will demand of him that he give our king his daughter in marriage, for the settled purpose of our king will not be denied."

"Very well," Faris nodded his grudging accord. "Come with me. Our king awaits your audience."

Together the two viziers left the rampart wall-walk and passed on straight into an undercroft—a solidly built stone-vaulted room buttressing other rooms in the loftier levels of the vast castle carved out of the mighty mountain cave above. Sauntering through a semicircular tunnel-shaped barrel vault they came directly to an arched doorway which opened out quite unexpectedly into the uppermost level of an enormous subterranean chamber. Down a lengthy flight of very long and wide flagstone steps, broken at regular intervals by even longer and wider stone platforms, they descended gradually into the deep chasm of rock—its craggy dome ceiling draped with long and tapering stalactites. Light filtering down fitfully from the cavernous opening above grew dim and shadowed by the torch firelight which gradually displaced it. Then the two viziers bent their steps along a screens passage—a long and tall arcade flanked by a series of shallow arches bolstered by big-based circular columns and capped by ornamented stone-block capitals—leading at its end to a decorative ogee arch which curved considerably from a hollow to a bulging shape. Clamorously their footsteps clattered with a monotonous echo across the hard and polished flagstone floor. Finally they drew near the arched gateway through which flashed and flickered a dazzling rainbow of brilliantly colored and scintillant light—Bahram approaching it with an expression of curious, expectant and perplexed awe.

"Behold—the great hall of the King of Pearl!" Faris announced ceremoniously.

Together they stepped up to the colossal arched portal and into the spacious inner ward at the heart of the great cave castle. Entering the great hall itself was like stepping inside the huge hollow of a gigantic and glassy tank-basin, for the mammoth cave chamber was carved out of thick and heavy quartz rock crystal—its limpid, bell-shaped walls radiating with beamy, iridescent sunlight shining down pendulously through the sea. Above, below and all around sunbathed seawater bled and pressed all over from outside the cavernous walls, pushing up against even the crystalline floor spreading wide beneath them. Through the lucent surfaces could be seen teeming schools of all manner of fish swimming in all manner of ways.

Surrounding the inner ward was a high inner wall-curtain of solid, rectangular-shaped masonry piers buttressing archways and a domed ceiling which enclosed the whole cavernous courtyard. A narrow battlement wall topped off the outermost upper edge fringing the inner wall-walk above. At the hall's far end was a raised dais and floor space upon which rested the large royal throne made of giant mother-of-pearl shell—its nacreous surface ablaze with a lustrous, rainbow-like sheen. Bright prismatic light from the encompassing sea cast its brilliant beams through the clouded crystal and across the glittering throne and the regal monarch standing alongside it.

Wearing a long silken robe embroidered with gold brocade and jewels and a gilded gold diadem set with pearls and jewels the King of the Isle of Pearl turned from his admiring gaze at the passing procession of teeming sea creatures to face the two viziers whose clattering footsteps he heard nearing from behind. Then he sat down upon his throne, easing himself onto its round velvet cushion, leaning against a gilded armrest cast in the shape of a golden seahorse, and awaited their approach.

Bahram knelt before King Freton, bowing and touching the floor and then his lips and his turban with his right hand.

"It is not seemly that a man bow and prostrate himself upon the ground before any but God—to whom belongs all honor and glory!—the Prime Mover of the heavens and the earth and all other things," the king mildly admonished him, gesturing for him to get up. "Arise, then, for you will not stand in attendance on me."

Bahram then stood up, bowing his head and body only slightly forward in salute.

"May your domain forever and always be honored and revered by your lordship, my king," he said with reverence.

"A friendly and free and ample welcome to you who have come to us!" the king hailed him heartily. "I am your servant. My city is at your disposal. And everything you ask for shall be done for you. Tell me then, my lord, what are you called and from what country you are."

"I am an emissary from the Land of the Red King—King Zahhak," Bahram proclaimed. "I am called Bahram and I am my king's Grand Vizier and High Priest and First Minister. I have come to your city as a friendly visitor—not to contend or cross swords. So if you will open up your door to me I will pay you a friendly visit. And if you do not admit me I will return and not molest you nor the people of your city."

"Nothing has brought you here but some pressing matter that has come to you," the king declared reassuringly. "And whatever thing you desire from my country I will do it for you."

"My king," Bahram related, "surely my case is wondrous and wonderful and it is this: the king of my country has become enamored of a certain portrait of a particular young woman."

"This is the cause of your coming to our country?" King Freton looked perplexed and puzzled. "By Allah I am lost in amazement, for this is a marvelous thing. I pray you to tell me fully whose portrait it is he saw and how this bears upon us here."

"Hear me, my king," Bahram pleaded urgently. "It has reached the ear of my king that you have a daughter and he wishes to demand her of you in marriage."

Suddenly King Freton looked shocked and taken aback.

"Yes," he stammered slightly, "but how did your king come by the knowledge of my daughter? And how did he come by his desire to demand her in marriage?"

"Know, my lord, that the King Zahhak saw a forbidden picture of her in the possession of an artist and by it my king's reason was captivated," Bahram recounted. "So he asked the artist of it and it was told him that a damsel of surpassing beauty and loveliness was once seen on this Isle of Pearl, and was said to be the daughter of the king of this island realm. And when my king cast his eyes on her portrait, emblazoned upon a palace wall, he became enamored of her and suffers the deepest affliction because of her. So at my king's bidding I took with me some of his wealth and came along, and my king craves of you your perfect generosity, and demands her in marriage for him whose portrait it is he saw."

Looking surprised and startled King Freton resigned himself to concede to the vizier's knowledge.

"Know, my lord, that the original model of this portrait is my daughter and I am her father and she is called Jamila, Princess of the Sea, for she is of the children of the sea, and there is not on the face of the earth a woman more beautiful than she," he finally confided with pride, but looking disconcerted and ill at ease. "She will not consent to any proposal of marriage, although many have already demanded her hand in marriage, and although her suitor may offer to lavish all manner of wealth upon her. Any such proposal of marriage would only make her enraged and she would send any suitor away with a broken heart. So respect her wishes and stoop to accept my excuses and take pity on my sorrow, for now you know that we cannot consent to your king's demand of her in marriage."

"My lord salutes you with all due respects," Bahram firmly reaffirmed, "but asks you how long the Princess Jamila will remain in your domain an unmarried damsel, for the time must become trying for her. What then is your design in not giving her away in marriage? And why do you not marry her during your lifetime like other damsels?"

"Because she is unlike all other damsels," the king answered sullenly, "because of her being a child both of the land and the sea, her parents being of mankind and of the Jinn, her worlds being divided between what is earthly and unearthly."

"My lord," Bahram persisted, his tone turning gravely adamant, "surely my king is perfect both in honor and valor, for he embodies all admirable qualities. And when the like of me demands a damsel in marriage of the like of you he lavishes upon you an honor, yet you spurn me with your lame excuses! Now—by the life of my head—you shall marry her to my king in spite of the nose on yours, for my king has bidden me not to return to him without her. And if it must be without your consent to take her by force!"

"Threats can be of no earthly use to you here," King Freton

said staidly, sounding saddened.

"Threats, perhaps not, but acts of power can most assuredly be of the utmost earthly use," Bahram retorted resolutely, abruptly crying out. "Behold!"

Bahram muttered under his breath and gestured demandingly to the hall's battlements before crying out once more—forcefully.

"Yield to me! Incline toward me!"

Awestruck King Freton watched as the battlements budged and started to slowly move—by sluggish degrees—the hefty stucco stones gradually bulging and bending far forward without breaking up.

"Now return!" Bahram commanded and the battlements grated gradually back into place, crumbling mortar dropping in splintery pieces to the floor.

"From where do you come by such power and might?" asked King Freton, stunned by the sight.

"How I come by it is not important," Bahram answered curtly. "That I am possessed of it is."

King Freton sat silent—stunned by what he just witnessed.

"King of the age," Bahram persisted, "your neighbor king craves alliance with you and will have me demand of you for him the hand of your daughter—the Princess Jamila. So do not disappoint me but accept my intervention, and whatever dowry you demand he will give you."

"The dowry—whatever it is—I would readily accept," King Freton said stoically, "but as for the Princess Jamila we shall have to take some time to think more on this."

"Time you may have, my great and noble and illustrious king, but not much," Bahram grudgingly allowed. "I have come to you on this matter which is productive of peace and prosperity and happiness for both you and your domain. I have come to you as an emissary to demand in marriage your daughter—renowned by her rank and lineage. And to that end my own king—who is endowed with great dignity and generosity—has sent to you many gifts and many rarities, craving your alliance."

Bahram paused to let the king ponder his words.

"Do you not then crave the same of him?" he finally asked.

"I pray you," King Freton replied, "sojourn with us this night and tomorrow we shall see."

"As you wish," Bahram grudgingly agreed, frowning with scorn.

"Rest then and take your ease in the palace where you took up your abode," King Freton, visibly relieved, invited him, "that the fatigue of your crossing may depart from you and tomorrow—if it be the will of God, whose name is exalted!—your affair will be completed in the most consummate way—by the will of God, the Lord of the heaven and the earth, and the Maker of all things!"

Again Bahram nodded his disdainful accord.

"It is well," he said, grudgingly resigned.

§

"My father, I have no mind to marry!" Jamila protested vociferously from her spot at the edge of the lucent green grotto-pool. "No, none at all, for I am a sovereign princess of the Jinn who rules over even most men, so I have no desire for any man who would rule over me!"

She sat in the shallows, her right knee poking up out of the water while her father knelt nearby upon the sand of the slender strand of beach.

"My daughter," the king sympathized, "know that I have been demanded—not asked—to give you in marriage to a magnanimous and valiant king of the land, for that he is the most excellent of mortals of his day—the most powerful and most exalted of standing—and noblest of rank. He suits none but you and you none but him."

"My father," Jamila's hands splashed the water with frustration, "if you mention marriage to me once more I will go into my chamber, take a sword and put its hilt to the floor and its blade to my waist. Then I will thrust myself against it until it pierces my back and so kill myself!"

King Freton stared down dejectedly at the sand his fingers etched in front of him.

"You threaten me as the king who demands you does."

"Who in this wide world of ours is able to threaten you, my father?"

"One who is versed in the black arts and possessed of the power of the Devil, as must be the Grand Vizier who the king sent to demand you for him, for I fear he is one of the hell-born: a sorcerer and magician!"

Suddenly more mindful Jamila looked careworn and worried.

"You have seen signs of his sorcery?"

"Yes, my daughter," the king answered seriously. "He moved the battlements of my palace to incline towards him and then return to their places—by no other means than the sheer willpower of his outstretched hands!"

"I have no use for marriage," Jamila insisted, her adamant voice full of menace, "for I shudder at the very idea of it with the deepest manner of hostility. And if you force me to marry I will kill him whom I would wed."

"Force is what I fear most," the king desponded, "for the emissary of this king threatens to wage war against our land should we refuse to consent to the marriage his king demands. But if you are determined not to marry there is no help for it."

"How true is the threat posed against us?"

"Imminently true, my daughter," the king answered gravely. "You know full well the hidden power we possess. I fear our two kingdoms will go to war, fall to swords and together our two peoples will go to wrack and ruin."

"If you give me to this king to wife you and he will be of one condition?"

"Yes—me and him would be as one body and we would both

be safe from each other, for he seeks alliance with us."

"Nothing remains then, my father, but that I wed and that we all be united."

"In very truth, my daughter, I fear as well that the same would come to you that came to others who married for the sake of cowardly expedience."

"What came to them, my father?"

"Life without dignity or self-respect, and finally death for want of true love and contentment, such as that your mother brought to me," the king mused. "So sit you still and say nothing and do not lay open your life to such pain and misery, for by God, I offer you the best counsel which comes only of my fatherly love and affection for you."

"Why do I see you so changed and oppressed with so much worry and anxiety?" Jamila asked, growing fearful. "By God, my father, how long will this threat of force last?"

"Until either our two kingdoms are united in marriage or until we defeat in war the king who demands you," the king answered solemnly.

"When must you give an answer to this demand?"

"We will discuss the demand in private audience at court tomorrow."

"Then I can neither sit still nor silent." Jamila turned stoical. "My father, I have no choice but to approach this king and be married to him."

"No," the king objected, "you will not do this deed just yet."

"Of a truth I will," Jamila insisted. "I must."

"No, my daughter," the king raised his dissenting voice, shaking his head. "I do not need your consent for me to marry you. But I do need to know and learn more of the king who demands you, for you can marry only a man who is of our faith. And as the Prophet has said, when a servant of God marries, truly he perfects half his faith."

"What kingdom does he who demands me hail from?"

"The Land of the Magians or the Red King known as Zahhak."

"Those of the fire cult pray five times a day just as we do," Jamila mused, "but to the Lord of Light, Mithra, instead of to the Lord of Creation, Allah! But like us even the Magian kings enjoy harems, so a Magian king already married—should I marry him also—would favor his first wife over me, for I could never claim my coming before her. She would always enjoy the highest rank and station. So could I not object to being given in marriage to a king who has already another wife?"

"Under our law perhaps but not theirs," the king lamented.

"My father, I cannot oppose you, my sire," Jamila reluctantly acquiesced. "So do as you will, for truly heartache and despair are at an end, and I am one of the number of the king's hand-maidens."

"My daughter," the king discerned his daughter's deep discontent, "I am exceedingly struck by all this just as you must be. But I suspect a deeper—and perhaps darker—motivation lies behind the king's ambition to join in alliance with us by marriage. I can only suppose that he designs by his marriage to you to preserve his kingdom from the Muslim onslaught, which even now encircles and closes in around it. But then..."

"Yes, father?"

"Perhaps the true design is not the king's at all but rather that of his Grand Vizier, Bahram."

"You distrust this vizier, father?"

"Severely, my daughter," the king answered ominously, "for he is of the number of the one-eyed ones and is blind of the left eye—an evil omen. As the poet has said, keep no company with the one-eyed but beware of his wickedness and treachery, for had there been any good in him God would not have caused the blindness in his eye."

"Then why not kill this vizier, father," Jamila asked zealously, "for does not the Book command all Muslims to kill idolaters where we may find them?"

"You ask a difficult and troublesome question," the king

heaved a weary sigh, "for there is much to ponder and consider. And you do speak the truth, my daughter, for the Book truly does command us to wage war against idolaters and kill them wherever we may find them, but only until they repent being the minions of the Devil and become one among the believers. This would hold true as well for those who would seek their safety and security from us by means of hostility."

"Then does not the way of Allah lie clearly before you?" Jamila asked eagerly. "Should you not pursue unrelentingly and fight harshly this idolatrous enemy?"

"My daughter," the king looked askance at her, "have I taught you so poorly? The Book commands us never to kill the life that Allah has made sacred except in the cause of justice and right, for it is the way of Allah never to initiate hostility, but to fight against only those who would first fight against us. For it is also written that God does not love the aggressor, and that whoever fights by aggression will be cast into the Fire."

"Then we are forbidden to kill the aggressor before he aggresses against us?"

"More, my beloved daughter," the king answered devoutly, "we are bidden to forgive the aggressor once he ends his aggression, for Allah is All-Forgiving, All-Compassionate and All-Merciful!"

"Will I tell you then what is in my mind to save both sides from ruin?"

"Say on, my daughter."

"I wish you would give me in marriage to this demanding king," she resolved, humbly hanging down her head. "Either I will live or I will be a ransom for the children of Moslems and the cause of their deliverance from his hands and yours."

"God on you!" the king bellowed. "How can you be so spare of wit and good sense? Do not risk your life to such peril! How do you speak to me in words so far from wisdom and so near to folly? Know that she who is in want of experience in worldly affairs falls easily into calamity and misfortune."

"You have no choice but to make me a doer of this good deed and empower me as it will happen," Jamila declared decisively. "I will only die a ransom for others."

"My daughter," the king asked, aggrieved, "and how will that profit you when you will have thrown away your life?"

"My father," Jamila answered in earnest, "it must be, come of it what will."

"My daughter," he refuted her, "not all believers should set out to fight to conquer idolatry—not even as a ransom for our Muslim cousins, for the Book tells us that some among the believers must remain behind—at home—to gain sound knowledge and understanding of their faith, so that they may warn returning messengers of the faith to take care and beware!"

"I shall never stay, my father, nor will these words change my purpose," she persisted. "Leave such idle talk. I will not heed your words, for if you deny me I will marry myself to him in spite of you. And first I will approach this king myself and alone and I will say to him, I asked my father to marry me to you but he refused, being resolved to disappoint his lord, begrudging the like of me to the like of you!"

"Does this have to be?"

"Even so."

"God," the king deplored vehemently, "do not make your father desolate and sick at heart by your loss!"

Abruptly he arose and plunged himself into the shallows beside her—careless of his flowing robes sloshing in the water, taking her grayish and sleek face into his warmly caressing hands. He stared, deeply penetrating her copper-colored eyes.

"My daughter," he said fervently, "all the treasures and hoards of the universe are not worth a single trimming of one of your nails. And he who hoards he hoards only from his soul. But you are my soul, Jamila. And I will pay this demanding king the dearest and most costly of ransoms before I will let you ransom yourself for our sake, for my soul—more precious than life itself—is beyond all price!"

Gently the king wiped away the tears welling and falling out over Jamila's soft and supple cheeks.

JOSEPH COVINO JR

NINE:
BATH OF LOVE

THE TABLE

"Believers, when you rise to pray wash your faces and your hands as far as the elbow, and wipe your heads and your feet to the ankle. If you are polluted cleanse yourselves. But if you are sick or traveling the road; or if, when you have just relieved yourselves or had intercourse with women, you can find no water, take some clean sand and rub your hands and faces with it. Allah does not wish to burden you; He seeks only to purify you and to perfect His favour to you, so that you may give thanks."—Surah V, 6

Jubilant shouts for joy resounded all across the calm inlet bay of the Isle of Pearl—its warm waters shimmering from the sky-climbing sun beating down so oppressively over it. Yusuf looked up from his place amidships on the small and frail wooden bark, where he hung over the side peering into a submersed glass-bottomed box looking for oysters resting upon the shallow, rocky seabed below. Rejoicing voices could be heard lustily chanting and grunting while a band of pearl divers stamped their feet and clapped their hands, their exuberance spreading swiftly among the scattered fishing boats—double-masted sambouks flying triangular lateen sails—dotting the expansive shallow water bay.

"What is the cause of so much celebration?" Yusuf asked curiously.

"They sing praises to Allah, for a diver has found a fine and precious pearl!" answered Malik, master diver, paddling water from the bark's back.

"Can you hear what they are chanting?"

"They say the pearl is like one of the stars of heaven—fit for only a king or a queen to wear—and that our reward from God will be rich!"

Kneeling erect and alert at the bow of the boat the stout tender, or rope-man, wearing a blue and red cotton sarong, abruptly interrupted them.

"My sheik!" he cried. "Our diver is making no more signals with his rope, which is slack and lifeless!"

Yusuf hastened to the rope-man's side, hauling his hemp lifeline until he yanked its tail end from the water. Worried, he snapped up and plunged into the water the glass-bottomed box to look about for the diver below.

"What do you see?" Malik asked anxiously.

Yusuf lifted up his eyes, grim-faced.

"Nothing, my shiek!" he reported gravely. "The water is clouded with sand! He must be in trouble and struggling! I'm diving in after him!"

Hurriedly he fastened his bone nose-pincher, seized a long pick-ended stick and, drawing in a deep breath, dove overboard, plunging himself into the limpid shallows.

"God be with you!" Malik cried after him.

Obscured by murk—the sea bottom clouded by churning sand below—the water grew darker the deeper Yusuf dove. Showing through the murky haze, squinting, he picked out the coarse-grained sand of the oyster bank stretching out beneath him. Formed of granite some forty feet below the surface the sand fused with profuse oyster shells cemented by corals and lime, glittering in the clear blue water turned translucent by the blazing sunlight shining from above.

Yusuf discovered the diver's rope oyster basket, lying discarded with its full catch upon the sandy bottom. Soon he spotted the true object of his search—his fellow pearl diver, flailing helplessly in the water, his sun-bronzed body writhing wildly in pain and frenzy. One of his legs was tightly clinched at the ankle in the monstrous jaws of a giant clam—its mammoth ribbed valves clamping down tenaciously around the diver's engulfed foot!

Yusuf promptly rammed his stave into the clamshell's tightly clenched jaws, heaving and wrenching it violently up and down until he gradually pried open the monstrous mouth, liberating the diver's bitten and bloodied leg. Once his fellow was snatched from the clamshell's jagged jaws of death Yusuf grasped him firmly round his chest and held fast as he crawled up towards the shadowed brightness looming above, choking convulsively for air.

Together the two burst the sparkling surface, gasping robustly to breathe, flung their weary arms across their bleary eyes and plucked off their nose-clips, water streaming from their heads and shoulders. Yusuf guided his fellow's groping hands to the side of the bark, patted his wet back and lifted up his grateful eyes to Malik.

"God is merciful! The Lord is merciful!" he panted in praise, treading water.

He steadied the injured diver as the stout rope-man reached down, heaved him aboard and let him sprawl, flagging, in the boat.

"I will go back for the stick," Yusuf told the rope-man as he once more fastened his nose-peg. "Haul me in when you feel me pull on the lifeline."

In accord the rope-man nodded as Malik leaned over the side of the bark to admonish Yusuf.

"Take care and beware, my son!"

"I will, God willing!" Yusuf smiled and squinted from the glare of the blazing sun before once more deeply drawing in his breath and dropping beneath the shining surface, holding fast to the ballast line, his body a sun-bronzed blur disappearing into the depths.

Once more Yusuf reached the scattered oyster bank and crawled along the sandy bottom, clutching at coral rocks with both eyes wide open until he wriggled his way to the strand upon which lay the lost oyster basket and stave. Just as he snapped up the fallen spear—the bottom's disturbed murk oozing up all around him—he belched out a convulsive gasp of air and bubbles, soundly startled at the sudden sight of Jamila, jinni of the sea, abruptly appearing out of nowhere and gently covering his hands with her own over the shaft of the spear. She hovered round and glided closer to face him, her copper-colored eyes glinting, her razor-edged teeth gleaming.

Gently Jamila took the long stick away from Yusuf and entwined its pick in the mesh of the rope oyster basket. She yanked the length of rope hanging down from the shadowy surface above and together they watched the long lifeline and basket get hoisted spiritedly from the shallows.

Gesturing excitedly to his throat Yusuf signed that he was choking to breathe and thumbed for them to swim to the surface. Jamila shook her head, waving her hand in dissent. She drew near and folded him in her arms, gently touching her lips

153

to his, bubbles of air gurgling before their faces. Surprisingly Yusuf felt revived and breathed freely. Jamila motioned for him to follow her and kicked off ahead of him, swimming with the effortless ease of an undulating eel.

Above the rope-man hauled the dripping oyster basket and tangled spear into the bark. Peering through the glass-bottomed box Malik smiled knowingly as he watched the two companions stroke out of sight.

Below Yusuf chased after Jamila's lithe and willowy form and together they thread their way along the sandy seabed and through the cutting coral reef. Soon something lurid and tall loomed ahead out of the deep blue haze as they moved toward it. As they came up to it Yusuf strained his eyes and made out some sort of black monolith shooting up straight and erect from the sea floor. When they drew near enough to touch it Jamila gestured for Yusuf to ascend its face. Side by side they slowly scaled the depths and the gloom above lighted up, turning brighter until they broke the blue water surface. Yusuf gasped, gulped a lungful of air and looked up at the tapering spire of stone towering out of the water, squinting to see, for their side of the monolith was inscribed with cuneiform writing and its top peaked in the pointed shape of a pyramid. Peering around its edge Yusuf saw the floating caravan of pearl-fishing boats drifting pendulously at some distance upon the bay, their divers diligently plunging for the pearly spoils of the sea. At the monolith's side the two tread water and Yusuf gazed admiringly at Jamila's glistening wet face.

"I should not have left my boat," he protested. "My mates will worry about what has come to me."

"Have no fear," Jamila reassured him. "They will not worry, for Malik already knows what has come to you."

"How could he?"

"I have already told him," she answered, smiling mirthfully.

"Why then have you brought me here?"

"To show you this," Her upraised hand caressed the monolith's smooth ebony black surface, "and to put us out of sight of the boats."

"Why must we hide from them?"

Unexpectedly her hand softly covered and caressed his, pressing up with him against the stone.

"Because I desire to be alone with you," Jamila's eyes explored his for impression, "for I have expected you, and I have not slept these past nights from my excessive longing for you."

Looking incredulous and confused Yusuf feigned being deaf to her words, glancing skyward.

"Why does this obelisk stand here?"

"It is a monument to the divers of our island."

"How does its inscription read?"

"*In the sea of changeable winds,*" she recited reverently, "*His divers fish for pearls. In the sea where the North Star culminates they fish for yellow amber.*"

Jamila smiled warmly and drew near to embrace him.

"Is it true you have come to me or is this but a dream?"

"I am but your servant," Yusuf answered lowly with downcast eyes.

"You are most welcome but not as a servant. Surely from the time when I first saw you neither sleep has been sweet to me, nor has food been pleasant."

"In such condition have I been," Yusuf confided with his head bowed down. He looked up and devoutly met her penetrating gaze, which stirred his profoundest feelings. "Why have you come to me?"

"I desire that you come into the sea with me that I may take you to my world for a time."

"My sister," Yusuf objected mildly, "you were created in the water and the water is your home and it does not harm you. But if you come out from it to the land will harm not come to you?"

"Yes, my body will dry up, the winds of the land will blow upon me and I will be no more."

"In the same way I was created on the land and the land is

my home. If I go into the sea the water will flow into my body and drown me and I will be no more."

"Do not be afraid," Jamila heartened him, "for I will give you my life's breath which will contain and keep you, and the water will not harm you even if you spend the rest of your life traversing the sea. You will sleep and wake in the sea and nothing will harm you."

"If this be so, no harm," Yusuf consented. "Give me your protection that I may draw breath from it."

"It is so."

"Then I put my faith in God."

Once more Jamila gently touched her lips to Yusuf's in a soft gurgle of bubbles, filling him with her invigorating, life-giving breath and together they sunk deep into sea. Even agape with wonder Yusuf drew breath from the water just as he breathed air from the land. Feeling vitally alive he tread the sea bottom below just as he tread the dry earthly land above.

Suddenly the familiar luminescent glow of lapis lazuli radiated throughout the depths, erratically shooting out its brilliant beams and enveloping the two in a blazing haze of underwater light. Jamila pointed, signing for Yusuf to sight something bursting out of the haze into full view. From the blinding light mightily emerged a giant manta ray—the creature Arabian divers call the devilfish—gliding as gracefully through the sea as an albatross through the air!

Reflected sunlight flitting across the creature's back the monstrous manta swept along elegantly through the water, hovering round the divers and swooping down slowly towards them. Swimmingly the manta waved mammoth fins and winged around the awestruck divers in a close and flowing circle. Jamila signed for Yusuf to follow her, kicking off ahead of him with outstretched arms. He rapidly paddled after her and, reaching out to grasp and hold fast to the manta alongside her, they were both drawn languidly into the darkened depths.

Clinging tight to the manta they floated smoothly over the

rainbow-like coral ruts and trenches spreading expansively beneath them. Soon the rugged and angular edges of a darksome and obscure but mountainous mass of rock cropped up out of the murky blue gloom looming ahead. A massive undersea wall of coral plummeted precipitously before them from the surface to the sea floor—its sheer face falling in a sharp and tapering canopy which sloped to its expansive base below. Opening out from the wall's fissured face was a cavernous, tubular canal and the mighty manta soared straight for the gaping black hole in the rock. Into a short and narrow tunnel bored through the rock—the luminescent light radiating from the manta's body brightly illuminating its roughhewn walls—the two deep-diving riders were directly drawn. Before long the manta emerged from the cragged chasm, and gently winged their way upwards once more.

As they slowly scaled the dark depths a sudden and startling alteration drastically transformed the whole of Jamila's dark and lissome form. Luminous beams of lapis lazuli light shot out from her lithe torso, streaking throughout the length of her willowy limbs. Yusuf looked aghast, bubbles gurgling from his open-mouthed lips, but before he could take the full measure of her wondrous transformation, Jamila suddenly drew near to fold him in her arms and press her lips inseparably to his, clinging to him with an unbreakable embrace.

Lost in the profound passion of Jamila's melting kiss Yusuf never knew the exact moment, but finally felt and saw her richly long and wavy black hair caressingly entwining his face in flowing strands as they burst out together from the surface of the water. Once the water streamed from their wet faces Yusuf blinked his eyes clear and saw that Jamila's metamorphosis was complete—and once more she took on the form of a human being.

"What do you desire of me?" Yusuf asked, breathlessly treading water.

"I desire this." Clinging to Yusuf's neck with one arm she

gently rubbed her palm into his chest and lifted up to him her resplendently amber eyes. "I desire your heart."

"Come." Gently Jamila tugged on Yusuf's arm.

Together they swam a short span to a nearby strand of beach, stepping up onto it once their feet touched the bottom of the shallows, reaching out their arms to steady each other. They watched the mighty fins flap at the pool surface like the wings of a great bird before the manta ray dove into the depths, disappearing into a whirling swirl of water and scintillant light.

Glancing around Yusuf found that they emerged from a vast placid pool of emerald green water and stood upon the dry sandy bank of a spacious sea cave. Its colossal domed chamber was buttressed by hugely gnarled columns of solid rock—a rainbow-like drapery of stalactites strung out all along the cave ceiling, stretching down to touch the sprouting array of stalagmites carpeting the cave floor. Around and beyond the chamber's gravelly beach the pool's glimmering green water emptied into a yawning hole in the rock wall which opened out to a narrow streamlet flowing calmly from the cave.

Yusuf gazed lingeringly upon Jamila's eye-filling nakedness and sighed softly with wonder. Jamila shyly hung her head down before lifting up her golden eyes to his, her face flushed and smiling.

"You are the only man beside my father ever to see my body," she quietly confided.

Slowly Jamila crossed her delicate arms over her surpassingly soft and supple breasts and turned abruptly away from Yusuf with a hushed gasp.

"Once when my father looked upon my nakedness and I was ashamed," she recounted without turning about, "he told me that it was only right and proper that he should be the first to admire me. Only..."

Yusuf stepped up close behind Jamila and rested his hands gently upon her velvety smooth shoulders, stooping to kiss softly the satiny white of her exposed neck.

"Only what?" Jamila's blushing cheek nudged tenderly against Yusuf's caressing lips.

"Only the next man to lay his eyes upon me should be the one who truly loves me—as he does."

Slowly, gently, Yusuf nuzzled against Jamila from behind and languidly slid his hands down along her silky bare arms— his fingertips brushing softly against the full, fleshy curves of her breasts before reaching down around her wide hips to her sleek stomach, passing up once more across her delicate ribs to stroke softly her heaving, swelling bosom. Abruptly and tightly both her hands clutched his.

"No Yusuf, I beg you!" she gasped, moving anxiously but mournfully away from him. "We cannot."

Nimbly Jamila stepped up nearby to the small flagstone platform upon which stood the large cane-work chair, taking and putting on the blue-dyed calico garment embellished with gold braid which was draped over it.

For a long, solemn moment Yusuf stood silent, looking dazed and bewildered.

"Come with me," she beckoned him.

Cheerily Jamila took Yusuf by the hand along a narrow stone footpath which meandered through a rugged, low-ceilinged cave passage and led to an arched entry. Yusuf stopped and pricked up his ears to listen curiously to the melodious but melancholy tones of a lamenting lute, echoing a long way off throughout the cave chamber.

"I asked a servant of the castle to play for us from a distant closet," Jamila answered his expectant but unspoken question.

"What is this place?" Yusuf intently inspected the entry.

"This is my hammam."

"A bath?" Yusuf exclaimed, smiling sardonically and sniffing the sweet-smelling scent of aloes-wood burning in censers fuming with fine lign-aloes. "Did not the Prophet say that whatever woman entered the bath was attended by the Devil?"

"All the earth was given to him, he said, and as pure, except the burial ground and the bath."

"How then shall we enter?"

"By offering up a prayer for God's protection against unclean spirits and by first crossing the threshold with our left feet." She entwined her arm through his.

"It is so," Yusuf smiled with a nod.

"I seek refuge with God from Satan, the accursed!" Jamila recited, waiting for Yusuf to voice his assent.

"I seek refuge with God from Satan, the accursed!" he chimed in.

Together they passed through the entry, crossing the threshold with their left feet first.

Endless beads of warm water popped out upon the glittering alabaster and carnelian walls as hot steam rose from heated fountains and tanks, wafting upwards to the spacious hall's high domed ceilings—luminous beams of light streaming down from little rounded and glazed apertures. Chambers were lined with tessellated mosaic pavements made of black and white marble and pieces of fine red tile.

"My brother," Jamila smiled engagingly, laying bare her back, "perhaps you will untwist my hair so I may enter the bath."

Yusuf stepped up behind her and untwisted her long, sable black hair, gently stroking and running his fingers deeply through her silky soft tresses.

"Yours is such beautiful hair."

Endearingly he draped her hair over her smooth bare shoulders and she turned around to face him.

"Put off your loincloth."

A cold water fountain stood at the center of the small antechamber—its walls lined with raised platforms and benches encased in marble, their seats furnished with cushions and mattresses. Draped over a rope hung across the chamber were a number of body napkins. Unhesitatingly Yusuf obeyed, laid his loincloth upon a bench and stood, waiting expectantly while Jamila took four napkins from the rope and wrapped them one by one around his loins, chest and back, winding the last one about his head like a turban.

"Enter the hammam and I will go in with you and rub you down with the glove," Jamila invited him.

"Truly," Yusuf took Jamila's velvety smooth face into his hands and gazed at her with adoration, "the very sight of your face glorifies the Almighty Artisan Who fashioned you and adorned you with such beauty and loveliness."

He stooped to kiss her but she pressed her hands firmly against his robust chest, pushing him gently—but resistant—away.

"I brought you here for the bath," she said with dejected, downcast eyes.

"What ails you, my Jamila?" Yusuf sensed troubled signs in her voice.

"I want you to love me but do not," she hung down her head but lifted up her imploring eyes, welling out with tears. "I am trying not to love you but I cannot help it."

"I cannot help but love you," Yusuf confessed, "for my only desire has been to see you again."

"It has been my desire also," she warmly took his hand. "Come."

Together they passed through another arched entry and stepped inside the main bath chamber. Composed in the shape of a cross the central and chief part of the roughly square chamber was its main apartment. At its center was a fountain of hot water, rising from a base encased with a seat of marble. In one of the chamber niches blazed a fire over which stood the boiler-tank holding and warming the water pouring down from a hole in the dome above. From another niche protruded two sidelong taps set side by side for hot and cold water with a small trough set beneath, and before which was laid a marble seat.

Yusuf sweat profusely from the steamy heat. Jamila meticulously unwrapped and discarded all his body napkins except the one covering his loins and silently seated him upon the raised pavement of the dais surrounding the main basin—out of which spouted a jetting fountain. Burning censers sweetly perfumed the chamber.

"Lie down on your stomach," she bid him.

Yusuf did so, stretching out prostrate but glancing around to watch her while she proceeded to crack the joints of his fingers, toes, neck and back. Briskly she kneaded his flesh, rubbing down his whole body with woolen bag-gloves pulled over her hands. Using a coarse earthen rasp she rubbed the soles of his feet.

"Extolled be the perfection of God—to Whom belongs all might and glory!" Jamila exclaimed. "Enter the bath."

Obediently Yusuf arose and plunged himself into the tank of soothing, warm water. Thoroughly Jamila soaped and scrubbed him with palm-tree fibers, washing his hair and whole body.

"Now I will shave you."

Affectionately she rubbed into his bristly beard a sticky lemon yellow substance, mirthfully contemplating his curious expression.

"This is the depilatory," she explained, "a paste compounded of yellow arsenic and quicklime which removes the hair with comfort and ease. It will cause your hair to shed by such simple means."

Gently Jamila rinsed him with handfuls of water and Yusuf rubbed his smoothened face, appreciatively covering and caressing her hands with his own.

"Why do you do this?"

"Must I have a reason for doing it?" Softly she caressed his sleek cheek, smiling warmly. "I do it because I want to do it."

"Surely this hammam is the seventh heaven of this world!" Yusuf exclaimed.

Jamila poured rose-water from a casting-bottle into the pool, swirling it about in the tank water and sprinkling his body with it, vigorously rubbing it over his chest, shoulder and arms.

"The bath is the goodliest of delights and the best of the

good things of this world!" she boasted, looking pleased with her deed.

"Rare," Yusuf exclaimed, reveling in the satiny touch of her hands flowing over him, "if all this is not a dream!"

Jamila held up a barber's looking-glass before his eyes so he could see his polished face.

"My God," Yusuf praised, rubbing his shaven chin with un-adulterated satisfaction, "bless our lord Mohammed!"

"May it benefit you and do you a world of good!"

"Allah benefit you!"

"Tell me," she asked him with yearning, "will you stay with me here?"

"Yes and yes again!" he eagerly answered.

"Put this on." Jamila coaxed Yusuf to stand and wrapped him in a long sleeping-gown made of brocade with a gold-embroidered hem. "Come."

Again she took him by the hand through another arched entry and into a smaller salon, leading him directly to a couch of Indian rattan with ivory feet and seating him by her side.

"Yusuf," she took a sealed flask from a table set with flowers and scented herbs, "what say you to wine?"

"Do as you will."

Jamila poured wine into two crystal cups, handing Yusuf his.

"May God lavish His favors upon you," she devoutly toasted him.

"May God favor you, my Jamila," Yusuf raised his cup to her, "for I do not doubt that all this is but a wonderful illusion."

They drained their cups and Jamila drew toward them a round tray covered by a round piece of embroidered silk upon which were set saucers of grapes and watermelon together with two covered cups of cut glass.

"Take some fruit and sherbet, my Yusuf," Jamila tempt-ed him, playfully pressing to his lips a slice of melon, "for the Prophet has said that whoever eats a mouthful of watermelon

God writes for him a thousand good works and cancels a thousand evil works and raises him a thousand ranks, for it comes from Paradise."

"Surely you have come from Paradise as does the drink of sherbet," Yusuf praised her, gently nibbling the slice from her fingers and washing it down with a swallow of sherbet, "for the excellence of the violet from which the sherbet comes is as the excellence of Islam above all other faiths."

"Only I fear my faith is weakening," Jamila said faintly, looking unavoidably downcast.

"Tell me what this talk means, my Jamila," Yusuf implored her, softly taking her cheek into his hand, "and what has shrunken your breast and troubled your temper."

Unthinkingly she nuzzled his caressing hand, taking it into her own, softly kissing his palm and lifting up her pleading eyes to meet his.

"Is it not true that God has preordained five things to His servants," she asked anxiously, "their time of life, their actions, their abodes, their travels and their portions?"

"Whatever is in the universe is by the order of God," Yusuf affirmed. "This is our faith."

"Then it has become destined that I depart from here," she confided sadly, "and nothing has kept me from doing that but my affection for you, for I can barely keep myself apart from you for one day."

"Depart?" Yusuf repeated fearfully. "Bound for where?"

Jamila heaved a heavy sigh, turning silent and sullen.

"What has come to you, my Jamila?" Yusuf persisted. "Tell me and hide nothing from me."

"I have nothing to hide, my dearly beloved one," she warmly pressed his hands into her own, her voice growing indignant. "If the palace of my father crumbled tomorrow I would depart without a single thought. If he has decided this vile thing I will sever myself from him, even though he will not consent to make provision for me, for my Lord will provide."

"Jamila, you must tell me what this talk means," Yusuf pressed her, "for I do not understand."

Again Jamila's large, almond gold eyes welled out with tears.

"My dearly beloved one," she murmured mournfully, "know that my father has been pledged by demand to give me away in marriage to the king of a wicked magician, who brought with him as gifts nothing but his evil sorcery! But as for me I will have none of him, and wish because of him that I had never come into this world!"

"The magician demands you in marriage, or his master, for most magicians make obeisance to one?"

"His king—the crowned head of a faraway land."

Stunned, Yusuf pondered for a long time the import of what Jamila confided; solemnly she stared at him.

"Have you not heard it said in the proverb?" he thought aloud. *"Like the fish of the sea the strong eat the weak just as the rulers of the land devour their subjects."*

Yusuf folded Jamila snugly in his arms; she nestled her head against his chest.

"Praise be to God Who has substituted for the fish of the sea this beautiful woman," he said consolingly.

Unexpectedly Jamila arose from the couch, spread a mattress over the floor and took Yusuf by his hand, leading him to it.

"Lie you down and take your ease, for surely you must be tired."

"With gladness," Yusuf joyously consented, "if only you will rest with me."

Jamila glared but smiled mirthfully as they laid down together, pressing close to each other's bosoms and entwining in each other's arms. Gentle tears spilled softly from her dark and languid eyes. Leaning upon his elbow Yusuf tenderly touched her wet face.

"Here we can fall in love, my Yusuf," Jamila said sorrowfully, "but we cannot make love."

"*Precious are the tears of angels that rain from the sky,*" Yusuf recited from a poem he remembered, "*which turn into pearls as they fall to the sea, for these are dewdrops from heaven.*"

Caressingly he kissed her parted, quivering lips, lingering to wallow in their deep warmth. Ever so reverently he touched with his fingertips the dotted mole adorning her right cheek, kissing it also.

"You are my precious pearl, Jamila, just as this drop of dew has fallen upon your face," Yusuf said after a breathless pause. "Only there is something else you must know."

"And what is that, my beloved one?"

"You must know that you already have it—for it is yours—and that you need never ask for it again."

"But what?"

"My heart."

TEN:
SEAL OF SULEYMAN

THE HEIGHTS

"We have predestined for Hell many jinn and many men. They have hearts, yet they cannot understand; eyes, yet they do not see; and ears, yet they do not hear. They are like beasts—indeed, they are less enlightened. Such are the heedless."—Surah VII, 179

JOSEPH COVINO JR

When Yusuf finally awoke from his deep and peaceful sleep, his head resting fast upon his arms, he felt Jamila gently rubbing and kneading the soles of his feet—the customary way of waking a sound slumberer. Calmly his leaden eyelids blinked open.

"I cannot help but think I have flown into Paradise or else I am in the transport of some fanciful dream," he muttered with delight, smelling the scent of musk which still effused from her.

"You slept well," Jamila smiled mournfully, "but we must go. It is almost dawn."

"Come," she rose to her feet, holding out her hands to help him rise to his.

Yusuf followed Jamila out of the hammam bath, back along the narrow flagstone footpath and through the cragged tunnel to the very edge of the strand of sand inside the great subterranean cave chamber.

"Follow me there," she pointed to the streamlet pouring into the nearby cave passage—its mouth yawning to swallow the spilling pool.

Suddenly Jamila cast off her garment and dove into the pool. Yusuf followed her, feeling refreshed and revived by the soothing water. Together they swam briskly along the darksome streamlet—the flowing current carrying them smoothly through the rounded, roughhewn passage. Soon they came to some emerald green shallows and climbed onto a smoothened shelf of stone, water streaming from their bodies. Again Jamila assumed the sleek, slate form of the sea-jinni.

"This way," she bid him, smiling at the stupor showing on Yusuf's confused face.

From outside a dim and faint light—a hazy sky blue—dispelled the gloom of the passage just as a distant and hollow roar diffused its still silence. Together they walked along the narrow stone ledge fringing the tunnel wall—thick slabs of rock bulging irregularly from its angular surface—soon coming to a rapidly cascading waterfall which thundered into the pitchy pool overflowing the cave's gaping mouth. Once they passed through, emerging from the opening beneath the tumbling falls and entering the open space of the expansive, cliff-lined cove and lagoon Yusuf spotted the familiar black Arab tent and knew instantly that they had returned to the place where they first met: the Harbor of Safe Refuge!

"You see," Jamila confided, "I have been close to you for a long time."

"Yes," Yusuf smiled knowingly at the revelation, "I do see."

Arm in arm they strolled slowly to the lapped edge of the white shingle and sand beach and stood close together in the gently ebbing tide, water swirling about their sunken ankles.

"Take care and beware, my Yusuf!" Jamila admonished him, glancing back to the mouth of the waterfall cave passage. "Never swim through the passage during the high tide, for the walls of the passage collide during that time—like two clashing giants—and would crush the life out of you should you be caught between them."

"I will heed your words," he assured her.

"Now I must leave you and go my way," she said sadly.

"No, my Jamila," he pleaded. "Do not leave me desolate."

"There is no help for it," she ruefully hung down her head.

"My Jamila," he gently embraced her cheeks with both hands, "when will I see again this lovely face?"

"How can you believe it is lovely now?" Softly he caressed its silvery lines.

"Because of the love it bears for me."

Tenderly their lips touched in a warm and lingering kiss just as the first light of day broke above the faraway horizon, shooting out its radiant beams all over the glimmering, deep blue sea.

"I will come to you at the beginning of this night," her eyes deeply explored his.

"Then do not delay," he implored her, "for I will be anxiously awaiting you."

Jamila nodded, turned around and dove into the rolling surf; and Yusuf watched her rapidly disappear beneath the billowing waves.

§

"Eight glories meet—all joined in you—by which Fortune is your servant and liegeman: preeminence, lordliness, grace, generosity, eloquence, dignity, honor and victory!" the visiting Grand Vizier, Bahram, exclaimed, hailing and saluting King Freton in his great crystal Hall of Audience.

"And you, who gives the royal state sweet savor, you are a vizier who will never fall from favor!" King Freton saluted him. "How are you, my lord? Has my island country pleased and delighted you?"

"In truth from beginning to end!" Bahram affirmed with praise.

Groaning, Bahram strained to lift before the king a crystal coffer and laid it at the foot of his royal throne. He laid open its lid, heaved out a casket hung with seven steel padlocks and plunked it down upon the crystalline floor.

"I have brought with me a gift as a sign of homage," he announced ceremoniously, "that I might show it to you with your sufferance."

"There will be no harm in that," the king allowed with a permissive wave of his hand.

Turning keys Bahram clanked loose the locks and broke open the casket, exposing a glinting heap of gold and silver coins ablaze with their flame-colored brilliancy.

"Although ours is not a trading race," he proclaimed, "we carry to you thousands of our gold and silver coins bearing the effigy of our great King Zahhak—the immortal man among gods and the most illustrious sovereign among men! This is precious little with which to honor and revere the lady Jamila, my lord, for she is worthy of these coins a thousand-fold."

"It is worthy of her," the king granted.

"Then we crave to pay her tribute and offer this modest treasure as her dowry—of which this casket is but a paltry part. And whatever else you desire of me my king bids me to give you."

"I accept from you all of them," the king graciously agreed, "but I make a gift of them to you, for nor are we a trading race of people."

In the same breath Bahram shook his head in pointed protest.

"Nothing is more fated to give affront and outrage than a Muslim giving back and refusing to accept a gift given him—is it not, my king?"

"Let go your demand of my dear one," the king firmly insisted, "for I am not in want of riches or wealth. Nor do I yearn for gifts of gems or jewels. I brought her up an infant upon the bed of fondness and surely I am grieving and troubled for her in mind."

"And what would you have me tell my king of your refusal to accept his gift and honor his demand?" Bahram asked with a frown.

"My vizier," King Freton solemnly admonished him, "go to your king and tell him I would accept from him his dower and stand by our contract of marriage, and that my daughter would be his bride and he would be my son-in-law, and that he would see nothing from me but all honor and respect—but for one thing."

"And what would that one thing be, my king?" Bahram looked gravely vexed.

"A Muslim woman wedded to Islam is forbidden to marry any man but one of her own faith."

"For our king to marry any woman outside of our own faith is also viewed with disfavor," Bahram objected, "but our king's desire to take the lady Jamila to wife is so violent that he bids me to tell you he is favorably disposed to convert his faith to yours."

"Only the lady Jamila thinks ill of a marriage to a sovereign king who already has a wife of superior rank."

"Superior but scarcely supreme," Bahram reassured him. "My king is minded to raise the lady Jamila to the highest and most exalted rank."

With a summoning wave of the king's hand a young page submissively approached the throne holding a round indigo blue velvet cushion upon which rested a sparkling crown of red gold—set with all manner of jacinths and jewels such that no portion of riches would ever be enough to trade for.

"And what do you desire now, my vizier?"

"I have told you time and again of my desire—and that of my king," Bahram's voice expressed growing vexation, "that he demands in marriage your daughter, the lady Jamila, and that he bids me to carry her back to our country by whatever means necessary—whether by persuasion or by force."

Tightly the king's hands gripped the sides of his throne as he glowered at the vizier, his own features betraying a growing anger, only his grip upon his throne relaxed as his anger gradually lapsed into surrender.

"One part of our holy Book gives us clear warrant to kill those who would seek their security from us by making threatening advances and holding out with their hands war instead of peace," the king declared, "while another part warns us not to kill one another or squander our wealth in vanity and conceit."

"Spare us both by not preaching to me your self-righteous piety," the vizier sternly demanded. "Just give me your answer."

Looking resolute and unruffled the king gestured gently to the anxious page standing at hand holding the spangled crown.

"My answer is before you."

"My vizier," King Freton boldly pronounced, "this bejeweled crown of red gold is a gift from me to your honored king. It will symbolize our joining in marriage and by it we will all become one kingdom. And every little while we will bring you the like of it, for these jewels are more plentiful with us than the pebbles upon our beach, and are so easy to us."

Lost in wonder Bahram drew near the timid page to reverently lay his hands upon the glowing crown.

"Tell me, what say you?" the king asked, prideful. "Have you ever beheld in your time such precious stones as perfect and pure as these?"

"No!" Bahram exclaimed, staring spellbound at the dazzling crown. "Never at all until this day have I beheld the like of these stones for their sheer size, symmetry and magnificence! Not in the land of the Red King! Nor do I believe that there can be found in our entire treasury the like of even the tiniest of these!"

Solemnly his fingertips caressed the crown's blazing diadem of rare gems and jewels.

"No, by the great god of the Fire!" Bahram exclaimed again with amazement. "Just one single stone among all these is worth our whole domain!"

Pressing his right hand to his breast Bahram bowed submission to the king with reverent salute.

"I am humbled before you, for you have dealt so generously with us, showing exceeding munificence and presenting us with this splendid gift, which the people of our land would be powerless to give."

"My vizier," the king declared, "you now have a claim on us. And we cannot help but do honor and pay tribute to you, for you have done honor and paid tribute to us by your demand."

"My king of the age," Bahram fervently affirmed, "if we stood on our faces in your service a thousand years about nothing else could we repay you enough, and our doing so would be but a small thing, and a bare pittance of what you deserve."

"I grant you then that which you wish and desire," King Freton raised a sanctioning hand. "But…"

"My lord?" Bahram lifted up his expectant eyes.

"There is yet something else I wish you to consider," the king waved a beckoning hand.

As the one holding the crown stood aside two other pages stepped up carrying a great chest of precious wood with locks and hinges of copper and steel, setting it down before the throne and moving well away. Surprisingly King Freton came down off his throne and stood before the chest, gesturing for Bahram to seat himself upon the floor.

"Sit yourself down with me on the carpet," he invited him.

Together they sat down facing each other, cross-legged, and the king broke open the great chest, exposing its inlaid interior shimmering with iridescent mother-of-pearl. Filling the chest's hollow were several cucumber-shaped jars of yellow copper whose mouths were stopped with leaden caps, stamped with the signet ring of King Suleyman—on whom be peace!—and bearing his sacred seal: two equilateral triangles crossing each other to form his six-pointed star! Before them the king spread over the floor a gold embroidered white cloth. Wielding a small knife he pried off the lead stops to several jars and handily spilled onto the cloth their confined treasure: lustrous and precious pearls! As more jars were emptied the bigger the pearls grew.

"Nothing on the cloth will change their creamy color," the king declared.

"You have put before us a pure paradise of pearls!" Bahram marveled.

"And now behold the greatest of my pearly treasure!" the king proudly boasted, drawing out from the chest a final jar from which he cast out the last, biggest and most lustrous pearl. "By itself this single pearl alone is more precious than all the others! It is my very own and I hold it dearer than anything in the world!"

Bahram picked up the precious pearl and held it up before his eyes, peering deeply into its nacreous luster as he caressingly turned it upon his fingertips.

"You have put in my hand the very soul of man!" he mused wistfully. "In legend the pearl is the divine spark which man has lost but always tries to recapture, for it comes from the glory of God."

"For that reason it is beyond price. And for that reason you need never pursue it again."

"What are the meaning of these words?" Bahram lifted up to the king his bewildered eyes.

"If you give up your king's demand for my daughter in marriage," King Freton told him bluntly, "you have my leave to carry away to your country the soul of man in her place."

"Then you propose to tempt and corrupt me!" Bahram glowered, looking annoyed and suspicious. "Or do you mean only to give me insult?"

"No, I mean you no insult," the king hastened to assure him. "I mean only to offer you a fair trade: your demand for my daughter in marriage in exchange for the pearl of man."

"Your offer of a trade is most fair, to be sure, but it is impossible for me to accept—at any price." Bahram put down the pearl, remorsefully shaking his head. "It is also impossible for me to remain here longer, for fear of my king. So I must go— and your daughter must go with me."

King Freton rose to his feet and stood firm; Bahram rose to face him.

"My lord," the king said stoically, "have patience with us until tomorrow that we may make preparations to perform the marriage-contract. Then we will come to terms and take our oath together."

"You have granted me favors beyond my power to acknowledge," Bahram affirmed, "and completely satisfied all my wants. I will thank you, then, so long as I live. And when I die my bones will thank you in their grave."

§

"I was exceedingly distressed by all this," King Freton told his dearly beloved daughter with care. "Scarcely was I certain that the light of day had appeared when I made haste to tell you."

"Tell me what, my father?" Jamila asked apprehensively.

Again they sat together at the edge of the slender strand of sand deep inside the hushed and shadowed grotto—its sunken chamber echoing with monotonously dripping water.

"The deed will be done tomorrow," the king said solemnly after a pensive pause. "We will perform the marriage-contract and we must keep our oath, for the Book warns us that if we swear by God we must not make Allah an obstacle to our making peace among men, for He knows what is in our hearts. And by our marriage our only intention is to make and keep peace between our two kingdoms."

"I will do my duty to God," Jamila promised.

"It is a difficult and forbidding duty to be sure," the king affirmed. "And had God willed and did as He pleased He could have given guidance and direction to every soul, but He chose instead to let every man guide and direct himself. And so you too must guide and direct yourself. And no one can guide and direct you best but yourself, for only you know best your own heart. But even so I want to give you something of God's own protection."

"And what is that, father?"

In answer the king carefully held up to the flickering firelight a glowing bezel finger-ring. Jamila examined closely the fine belled, red stone ring and discerned that its blazing gem bore the six-pointed star: the Seal of Suleyman!

Its high bezel design displayed a heavily encrusted and richly decorated relief in the shape of a flower. Six turquoise petals encircled a brilliant red garnet set in the middle and held by claws with vivid orange red carnelian stones set on each side. With verses the cast ring band itself was ornately inscribed. Gingerly the king held out the ring to Jamila who took it and read aloud its inscription.

"*My Lord,*" she recited, "*bless and favor me that I might join with you by your grace, for by Allah I will never desert or forsake you.*"

"This is only one of many such rings that King Suleyman engraved with his all-powerful seal," the king recounted. "And it commands one of the jinn who has heard and heeded the revelation of the Koran, and who by sacred scripture has been guided to the truth of the right road."

"Father," Jamila reverently turned the ring in her fingertips to intently gaze upon the garnet's shining six-pointed star, "tell me more of King Suleyman and the jinn who were in his power."

"King Suleyman, the son of David, was the divinely inspired and guided monarch of the whole world," the king continued. "By his seal he had absolute and unlimited power over all the armies of the jinn. They were at his command by the grace and favor of his Lord. And any of them who turned away from his command tasted the punishment of the flaming fire. His own seal-ring, upon which was engraved the most great name of God, came down to him from heaven. It was composed partly of brass by which he stamped his commands to the good and believing jinn; and partly of iron with which he commanded the evil and unbelieving jinn. Those of the jinn who remained obstinate in their infidelity he confined in brass bottle prisons which he stopped with lead and stamped with his seal. But those of the jinn who remained constant and loyal to the true faith he compelled to obey and serve God, for the jinn—like man—were created only that they might praise and glorify God. Surely this signet ring will preserve you from every trial if you fall into calamity or evil turns in time. It will cast off from you all hurt and harm, and help see you through any ordeal by a strong and powerful force wherever you may be."

"Do you mean by these words that the invincible might of the jinn is truly under its control?"

"Truly, my daughter," the king nodded at her. "This ring will win for you any wish, for it conjures a powerful servant called Kasif—so named after the earsplitting thunder. And whatever you have a mind to of the desires of this world rub this ring and its servant will appear and do all you command of him."

Expectantly Jamila glanced at her father and gently rubbed the king's bezel.

In a breathtaking blaze of bright light a bolt of lightning abruptly shot out from the ring's stone, cracking in a jagged flash of fire to the cave ceiling. Shattered rock crumbled and dropped down from above, plunking into the grotto pool. Materializing from this dazzling streak of light—lapis lazuli in color—was a levitating and transparent shape which was slowly assuming the appearance of human form. Monstrous in size the ring-jinni's crest touched the chamber vault and his feet wafted over the water. His head was like a dome, his hands like pitchforks, his legs as long as masts and his mouth as gaping as a cave. His gleaming teeth were like mighty millstones, his flaring nostrils like ewers, his eyes two blazing torches and his look fearsome and glowering. His thunderous voice boomed with an earth-shaking rumble.

"Peace be with you, vicar of God," he addressed the king with a reverent salute.

"And with you also be peace and the mercy of God and His blessing," the king saluted him.

"My lord and master! Ask what you will and it will be given you. Have you a mind to populate a ruined city or to devastate a populous one? To slaughter a king or to vanquish an army?"

"This, my daughter Jamila, has become your ruler," King Freton stood up to gesture to Jamila who stood aghast at the sight of the floating colossus. "You will serve and obey her and do her bidding loyally. She is your lady and mistress. Kiss her hands and do not oppose her but make obeisance to her—white and black."

"Daughter of my master," the ring-jinni bowed, raising his

right hand to his breast, "if anything makes you fearful, or anything disagreeable comes to you, or any longing takes possession of you, rub this ring and summon me. And I will come to you quickly and do your desire."

"Return now to the ring," the king commanded him, "and be at the beck and call of your mistress when she sends for you."

Silently bowing and saluting the jinni's feathery and flimsy figure flashed and shot back to the bezel of the ring in a blinding blaze of brilliant blue light.

"By God," Jamila cried, "this is a strange and wondrous thing!"

"A powerful and unconquerable thing," the king seriously admonished her with portentous words of parting. Taking her hands into his he pinched the ring and held it up before her eyes. "Rub this ring and the servant will appear and do whatever you demand, for he will not dare defy you. Now to your destiny and take care of the ring, for by means of it you will oppose and conquer your enemies. But never be mindless of its power, for whoever fails to bear in mind her final cause and purpose in life loses the world as a friend. And only the vile and ignoble say I was lying at my ease and nothing but shamelessness brought me discontent."

"My father," Jamila hung down her head spiritlessly, "with your leave then I will go my way."

Unexpectedly the king pressed the ring back into her palm and held her hands even more tightly than before.

"My daughter," he implored her, "you must always keep this ring hidden and out of the sight of mortal men."

"But why?" Jamila looked curiously taken aback. "Is it not beautiful for any to behold?"

"Yes it is, my daughter. But it is also possessed of yet another very dangerous and deadly quality."

"And what is that, father?"

"If ever you wear this ring and raise your hand to point toward someone," the king answered gravely, "it will instantly strike off their head with a bolt of lightning."

ELEVEN:
SWORD OF JUSTICE

THE COW

"Righteousness does not consist in whether you face towards the east or the west. The righteous man is he who believes in Allah and the Last Day, in the angels and the Scriptures and the prophets; who for the love of Allah gives his wealth to his kinsfolk, to the orphans, to the needy, to the wayfarers and to the beggars, and for the redemption of captives; who attends to his prayers and pays the alms-tax; who is true to his promises and steadfast in trial and adversity and in times of war. Such are the true believers; such are the God-fearing."—Surah II, 177

Suddenly the ground all around Yusuf palpitated and rippled at his feet as he mindlessly bent his steps toward his black Arab tent. Lashed to fury from beneath countless gritty grains of sand, densely clouded and smoky, explosively blew up into Yusuf's face, severely biting and stinging his exposed skin. Out of nowhere four pairs of gigantic and wildly flapping wings—roughly triangular in shape and covered with colorful hair and scales—abruptly sprang up high on either side of him, forcefully fanning the fluttering strand of sand surrounding him. A monstrously oblong and elongated shape shattered the earth underfoot, heaving up from beneath the granular surface. Yusuf gasped, standing aghast as he watched two long and flexible antennae—hairy, segmented and threadlike—keenly prod the air with their acutely sensitive and knob-tipped feelers. It was a giant Paradise Birdwing butterfly, boisterously bursting out of the very seaside strand Yusuf trod upon.

Mammoth and magnificent the spirited insect erectly raised up brilliantly colored wings—their layered and overlapping scales imbued with iridescent splotches of blue and reddish hues. Underneath Yusuf felt a tremendous throbbing as blood pulsated convulsively through a large vessel running the full length of the insect's monstrous back, glistening with a bright and lustrous metallic sheen. He stumbled and fell headlong when the colossal creature lurched to raise up on three pairs of stout and jointed legs, swiping mightily at the air. Monstrous wings—both front and hind—beat violently and in unison.

Screwing up big globular eyes—set to the sides of the head but below the antennae—the giant butterfly coiled up the snakelike and spirally entwined proboscis beneath the huge head and body. Gradually the butterfly wafted from the ground and climbed skyward. Once aloft the butterfly arose, treading a fitful and erratic path up the steep face of the cove's seaside cliff.

Dazzled by the iridescent radiance of the vibrating striations and granulations of the butterfly's vein-etched wings Yusuf caught only fleeting glimpses of the plummeting seacoast and the soaring sea-cliff as he was hoisted swiftly in a zigzagging circuit to the towering mountain summit. Hovering level over the lofty land the butterfly abruptly reared up, Yusuf lost his groping grip, slid uncontrollably down the long luminous back and slipped helplessly into space.

He tumbled and rolled roughly onto a grassy, green spread of ground and watched intently—utterly dumbfounded—as the giant butterfly sporadically winged away aloft until lost to sight amongst the clouds. Getting strenuously to his feet he was at once amazed at the wondrous sight sprawling at length before him: a garden terrace and richly gilt gateway.

He strode directly to the edge of a spacious and brimming pool fed by water rising gracefully from the spouting plume of a central fountain and a soft waterfall spilling in serrated sheets and flowing over sloping gradients from its gushing fountain-head. Pensively he contemplated the balustrades, red sandstone walls and willows reflected in the pool's gently rippled surface and intently listened, taking in the quiet trickle of water, the frenetic buzzing of bees and the breezy swish of windswept chanar leaves.

Close to the fountain pool stood a decorative, twin-leafed garden gateway; Yusuf stepped up to read aloud the inscription engraved upon its richly gilt panels:

My God, I never listen to the voices of the beasts or the rustle of the trees, the splashing of the waters or the song of the birds, the whistling of the wind or the rumble of the thunder, but I see in them a testimonial to Your Oneness, and proof of Your Perfection, that You are the All-Prevailing, the All-Knowing, the All-True.

"You can never deny the Lord's bounty when the greatness of God lies all around you," professed a familiar woman's voice.

Stunned, Yusuf spun around to greet Fatima the devotee.

"Or when the butterfly of red rubies carries you off to the

heavenly gardens," he jested, striding over to salute the devotee, reverently kissing her hand and sleeve. "Peace be on you, my aunt!"

"On you be peace and the mercy of God and His blessings!" she saluted him. "Enter this Garden of Delight in peace and safety, for the word from a Merciful Lord for good deeds is peace!"

Yusuf followed Fatima and together they passed through the ornate portal—its gates grinding abrasively on their hinges.

"It has been said that music is made by the creaking doors of Paradise," Fatima affirmed.

"Would that not depend upon whether you heard the doors being opened or closed?"

"Perhaps," she showed an ironical smile, "depending as well upon which side of the doors you were."

Fatima's garden was a spacious green expanse of grass, flowers and trees spread in terraces upon sloping ground, closed in by balustrades and walls, carved and crisscrossed by running water canals, channels and chutes—all set out in a flowing framework of expansive courtyards and esplanades. Leafy bushes, shrubs and trees overhung the edges of narrow footpaths and neatly patterned parterres and stepping stones.

"The Garden is eternal," Fatima marveled, "like the earth and the sky where neither withering heat nor shivering cold has any place."

Together they trod a path through varying levels of ground—marked at intervals by a sporadic seat of stone—stepping up past a row of trees and a slanted plane of tumbling water. Flanked by paths and fringed with trees the main watercourse rose higher than even the surrounding floral carpets. Paths and terraces were paved with brick, worn sandstone and smooth, richly veined marble with slender strips of grass showing between pebbles. Lining the shady lane through which they strolled were twin rows of evergreen Cyprus trees and clumps of myrtle bushes heavily overgrown with creeping vines. Blossoming clusters of jasmine and roses overspread the flat grassy spaces—being bunched in earthenware pots and vases or planted in parterres—filling the air with their sweetened scents. Flitting nightingales sang their melodic songs. Quietly they thread their way alongside a coursing channel, passed over a smoothened stone path, climbed some stone steps and crossed a spacious lawn and stone platform set out with more blooming flower beds and slender stones.

"My aunt," Yusuf asked, "how did you know I was coming to you at this hour?"

Abruptly Fatima stopped to face him.

"It is time you took to wear your Dress of Honor," she said solemnly. "And I will give you a Dress of Honor such as no sultan ever dreamed of giving his lieges."

Yusuf looked incredulous.

"How is it that you have judged me deserving of this honor?"

"Because He whose name is exalted has said—in The Excellent Book—that those who ward off evil will walk among gardens and springs."

"Do you mean that which is promised to the defenders against evil—the Garden of Immortality?"

"Yes, my son," Fatima bowed with a nod. "It is both their destination and their reward."

"But surely," Yusuf objected mildly, "for those who ward off evil the reward of the Garden comes at the journey's end. Only I have endured none of the ordeals of battle."

"If ever you fear your imminent fate," Fatima heartened him, "trust all to Him who made the world and wait, for what Fate says must be: is! And you are safe from anything undecreed of Fate, for Allah is aware of those who ward off evil."

Fatima stooped and plucked from an earthen jar full of pink, red, white and yellow roses a single red rosebud and handed it to Yusuf, delicately fingering its prickly stem.

"Like Divine Grace grants the naked thorn its robe of honor

I grant you this red silken rose."

"Do you propose that I should wear this rose as my robe of honor?" Yusuf stared at the flower, mystified.

"The thorn boasts of its sharp weapon by which it protects the lovely rose against its host of enemies or against intruders who are not worthy of its scent. That is why the rose—moved by the fidelity of the thorn—gives the thorn its grace."

"Would I fight off evil with such a frail and fragile weapon?" Yusuf asked scrupulously.

"Whatever needful thing you undertake, my Yusuf, consult the knowing and the wise without contradiction!"

Yusuf looked profoundly perplexed as he watched Fatima reach into her fine silver waist-belt set with precious stones, drawing out from it a small camel leather purse with an indigo-dyed neckband. Silk tassels dangled from the purse's colorfully weaved, silver-beaded fringe. Carefully she uncoiled from her purse a glinting gold chain which ended in a terminal, mace-shaped pendant bead of pure black-and-white onyx. Yusuf bowed as she gently hung the gold chain about his neck. In his fingertips he caressed the onyx bead and discerned the six-pointed Star of Suleyman carved in relief as a cameo. In the star's topmost cusp the gold chain ended with five graven figures cut and jutting from its other five points.

"Tell me the virtues of this bead, my aunt," Yusuf craved, "and from where it comes."

"This bead of onyx is from a charmed treasure and possesses five virtues which will serve you in the time when you need them," she recounted. "My grandmother, mother of my father, was an enchantress who solved mysteries and carried off treasures, and from one treasure this bead came into her possession. And when my grandmother fell sick she made me a gift of this bead and acquainted me with the five virtues which it possesses."

"But what evil have I to fight off, my aunt?"

"A sorcerer who is blind of the left eye and who has come to demand in marriage for his king the Princess Jamila, the jinni of the sea," Fatima answered seriously. "This man is one-eyed and an evil omen. And of such a person the poet has said: keep no company with the one-eyed for even a single day but take care and beware of his wickedness and treachery, for had there been any good in him God would not have caused the blindness in his eye."

"From what kingdom does this sorcerer come?" Yusuf turned away to avoid betraying his suddenly pained and heart-sick expression.

"From the Land of the Red King, Zahhak."

"Has Jamila's father consented to this demand?" Yusuf's uncontrollably quivering lips gave utterance to the words grudgingly.

"As sure as fate," Fatima answered with a solemn tone, "his consent approaches."

"It has been said of Fate," Yusuf mused grimly, "that no man will entrust his weight to a rope except for a cause which calls for a rope."

"Surely you will be tried and put to the test," she gave him ominous warning, "but if you persevere and ward off evil then that is of the steadfast heart of things."

"How will I persevere against the evil growing in my own heart?" Yusuf turned about to face her, looking grievous and downcast. "How will I be rightly guided against that?"

"There is the Sacred Scripture of which there is no doubt," Fatima assured him. "Because Allah has endowed the Scripture with Truth it is the only guidance to those who ward off evil, for only in Scripture has Allah shown the Truth. Those who have heard the Scripture know that its Revelation is the Truth from their Lord. And they recognize it as they would recognize their own blood relations."

"What if I am tempted to do my worst and commit the evil which lies in my heart?"

"Allah shows to you the Scripture with His Truth that you

may judge and choose between that which is weak and human and that which is almighty and divine. You must not be a defender of the treacherous."

"Can Scripture keep me from becoming one among the treacherous?" he asked, despairing.

"This is a blessed Scripture which Allah has shown," she admonished him. "Follow it and ward off evil that you may find His guidance and mercy, for it will guide you to the Truth and the right road."

Onward they passed by a brimming, straight-sided pool bordering the courtyard garden fed by water flowing through clay, marble and stone channels—decorative chevrons adorning the channel floors. Mushrooming water trickled from the pool's splashing fountain. Rose petals were strewn and cast adrift across the pool's shallow but murky surface which reflected the sky's brightness and the scattered clouds drifting swimmingly overhead together with the surrounding colonnade. Set in the middle of a spacious patio the pool was a uniform pattern of paved slabs stretching across the wall-enclosed courtyard.

Fatima sat down upon the pool's hard-surfaced, elaborately carved edge raised above ground level. Smoothly she ran her palm over the mosaic tile pavement and white marble inlay, tracing with her fingertips the complex curvilinear pattern of intertwining floral designs, star shapes and surpassingly stylized rosettes.

"You must always remember, my Yusuf, that everything was created to worship God and everything praises God with its own voice. The growing of trees, the humming of bees, the scent of flowers—everything created utters unending praise of God. Listen and you can hear their praises."

Silently they took in the low murmur of water and soft rustle of leaves as the gentle sea-breeze swept over the mountain top; and flashes of dappled sunlight reflected from the pool's sparkling, pendulous surface, illuminating the encircling arcade. Fatima reached into the pool's still water and let a stray rose petal float gently into her hand.

"By their very color, fragrance and shape the flowers of the garden sing in mute eloquence their never-ending praise," she mused, arising to turn in her fingertips the fragile rose petal. "Like the angels whose only calling is eternal worship every plant in the garden devotes itself to prayer and the remembrance of God. Truly even the trees open up their branches in prayer and lead the adoring chorus. So you too must give praise, my Yusuf, and pray for God's intercession. Come."

Together they sauntered around the outer edge of the court-yard until Yusuf saw showing through the treetops a shining dome of turquoise tiles rising high above the gold of surrounding marble roofs and walls—their polished surfaces deeply grooved and engraved with ornate starbursts and star clusters. Its drum was pierced by an intricate grillwork and surmounted the holy mountain mosque. Finally they rounded the full length of the courtyard and came to a towering, free-standing minaret shooting up from its broad square base—a tapering, whitened cylindrical column ringed by decorative collars and topped by a massive capital which soared into the bright blue sky above. Winding round the entire length of the minaret was an unbroken spiral stairway which turned and twisted its way to the very top.

"It is a true place of prayer," Fatima marveled, mindlessly fingering the lustrous black coral beads hanging down low from her neck, "a fitting place for the Faithful to adore the Eternal!"

Slowly they crawled up the gradual and progressively sloping stairway, picking their way step by step until they rose to the height of the surrounding treetops. As they stepped higher up by slow degrees Yusuf could see once more showing through the foliage fleeting glimpses of the turquoise dome—and something else on top of it—a glinting figure ablaze with the radiance of sun-spangled brass: a mounted horse soldier and warrior, sitting astride his rearing warhorse-courser of brass with his pointed pike of brass in hand!

"Behold!" Fatima grandly proclaimed, "our brave and valiant knight of old: Antara!"

Abruptly a blustering flurry blew up around them as lowering clouds spread over them a vast somber shadow.

"Come," Fatima bid Yusuf again, leading him farther along up and around the twisting and encircling stairway. Soon they could command a breathtaking view of the precipitous cliffs plummeting below and the great bounding sea spreading far and wide before them, stretching to the uttermost parts of the earth. Once they reached the topmost point—the minaret's pointed peak—Fatima turned abruptly about to face Yusuf squarely.

"God has said by the tongue of His Prophet," she cried out as boisterous gusts wildly tossed her flailing veil, "that whoever surrenders his purpose to Allah while doing good his reward is with his Lord! And no fear will come upon him nor will he grieve!"

Yusuf looked aghast as Fatima took both his hands and clenched them tightly in hers.

"Say!" she cried again. "Will you choose for a protecting friend other than Allah—the Creator of the heavens and the earth—who feeds and is never fed? Say you are called to be of the first to surrender to Him!"

Tugging at Yusuf to press forward Fatima picked their way farther up the tightly tapering stairway upon which space to stand rapidly shrank and slipped away. Fearfully hugging and grazing the smooth, circular wall Yusuf was astonished at Fatima's unshrinking calm as they deliberately scaled the spare and slippery heights of the heavens. Sinking swiftly below were the widening ledges of the entwining spiral stairway, uncoiling sinuously to the distant ground.

"Of that which He has created," Fatima cried aloud, "Allah has given you shelter from the sun! And has given you places of refuge in the mountains! And has given you coats to ward off the heat from you! And coats of armor to save you from your own foolhardiness! Even so He perfects His favor to you that

193

you may surrender to Him!"

She guided his trembling hands to the very crown of the minaret's conical spire from which projected the upright hilt of a pikestaff.

"Lay hold of it, Yusuf!" she commanded him unflinchingly. "And hold fast to it!"

Yusuf did so, wavering, and the hilt suddenly began to glimmer and glow with a beamy and bright stream of lapis lazuli light. He winced from the dazzling glare and drew back but Fatima steadied him.

"Do not falter!" she bellowed. "Draw it out!"

Tightly gripping the protruding hilt—gilt with interlaced silver strap-work, a square- sectioned iron pommel and jewels—Yusuf drew out from the spire's tip a straight, double-edged Arab long-sword—a famed Damascus blade—forged of fine iridescent and watered steel with forty bars crisscrossing its entire length!

"Mohamet's Ladder!" Yusuf gasped, staring spellbound at the gold Islamic inscription embellishing the gleaming blade which he held up firmly before his face, reciting solemnly. "If you risk your life to gain a life you must answer in the presence of God for any death you cause, rightly or wrongly."

Abruptly a blazing firebolt shot down from the dark, lowering clouds gathering overhead and explosively struck the tip of the cutting blade with a deafening peal of thunder. Yusuf convulsively flinched at the brilliant flash of lightning and the stormy blast which smote his face.

"Strive in the way of Allah with the endeavor that is His right!" Fatima fortified him. "For He is your Protecting Friend! A blessed Patron and a blessed Helper!"

"Now has come to me light from Allah and a clear Scripture!" Yusuf exclaimed.

"Yes, my Yusuf!" Fatima looked conspicuously pleased. "Only there is something else you must always remember."

"What is that, my pilgrim?" Yusuf gazed aghast at the blazing blade.

"A poet has said that whoever lives in fear of the ways death may come death will yet kill him even though he aspire to climb to heaven upon the rungs of a ladder." She tightly clasped his hands with hers about the glittering hilt of the sword. "But God has said by the tongue of His Prophet that whoever kills a human being wrongfully it will be as if he had killed all mankind. And whoever saves the life of one it will be as if he had saved the life of all mankind! And so I implore you, my Yusuf, you must pray and give praise to Allah!"

"My Lord!" Yusuf cried, shuddering, and lifting up his eyes reverently to heaven. "You are my Protecting Friend in the world and the Hereafter! Make me die submissive to You and join me to the righteous!"

Unexpectedly another flashing streak of lightning shot down and struck the Arab sword, bolting across the roof of the mosque sprawled below and straight to the turquoise dome, hitting with a fiery blaze of lapis lazuli light the raised lance of spiked steel held by the brass warrior-knight: Antara.

Startled, Yusuf spun and fell prostrate, watching with wonder as the majestic horse soldier of brass, wholly ablaze with scintillant light, grudgingly came to life and began to move!

"Praise be to God!" he cried.

Then the pouring rain finally fell.

JOSEPH COVINO JR

TWELVE: GARDEN OF PARADISE

REVELATIONS WELL EXPOUNDED

"Among His signs are the night and the day, and the sun and the moon. But do not prostrate yourselves before the sun or the moon; rather prostrate yourselves before Allah, who created them both, if you would truly serve Him."—
Surah XLI, 37

A twinkling tapestry of stars overspread the lofty vault of heaven and sprinkled their glittering light across the blue-black night sky. A fanning spray spouted gracefully from the central fountain. Sparkling falls cascaded into the garden basin, tumbling smoothly like a sleek sheet of curved crystal, spilling easily over carved niches bearing earthenware vases of flowers and glowing lamps. Mirroring themselves in their own flittering light—together with that of the bright full moon beaming far off above—tiny rafts bearing flickering candles floated and scattered across the still surface. Silhouetted against the pitchy skyline but aglow with the luminescent light at the uttermost edge of the world sculptured trees cast their tortuous shadows across the glimmering, brimming pool. Through their feathery leaves the whistling breeze whisked gently along as the lush fragrance of pale flowers and perfumes sweetly scented the cool, quiet air.

At the pool's elevated edge—inlaid with its smooth and richly veined marble—Yusuf sat utterly alone. Fast by him sat a low-lying stand bearing an open Koran—The Book—alongside an outspread prayer carpet. Only instead of doing his devotions Yusuf brooded, obliviously tracing with his fingertips the infinite waves of a single vine tendril emblazoned in the mosaic tile—its curling branches, leafy scrolls, loops and spirals interlacing endlessly in their ever flowing rhythm.

Hearing a faint footfall upon the pavement behind him and a glassy tinkle of bracelets Yusuf wheeled about expectantly. His anxiety happily relieved he arose hurriedly to stand breathlessly spellbound at the sight of Jamila, jinni of the sea, standing demurely before him in her comely human form, wearing her blue-dyed calico garment embellished with gold braid and smiling delightedly back at him.

"The Celestial Garden is where heaven meets the earth and God meets man," she intoned with certain serenity.

"And where man meets woman?" He looked on her expressively. "Praise belongs to God."

"The place of Paradise is the place of reunion with your be-loved," she drew languidly near him.

"If there is a Paradise on earth it is here before me," he took her soft, flushed cheeks into his caressing hands, "for it is your face."

Their lips softly touched—warmly, tenderly—as they kissed. Reluctantly she turned away from him, looking deeply afflicted.

"What ails you, my darling Jamila?" Yusuf asked worriedly. "Has it not been said that you can see God's beauty by looking at water, greenery and a lovely face?"

"Truly," Jamila smiled sedately, "these are the things the Prophet said make a heart live long. Only the real gardens are found within man's heart—not without. And man's heart is like that of the tree, for if it is never moved to dance by the soft spring breeze of love it is sapless and loveless, and so doomed to become firewood."

She stooped to pick up a floating rosebud from the hushed fountain pool.

"Anyone who longs to look on God's beauty should look on the red rose," she mused, "for it is a blessing sent from Para-dise."

"You are a blessing sent from Paradise and I long only to look on your beauty, my beloved."

Jamila humbly hung down her head.

"Did you know my name means beautiful?"

"I knew without knowing."

"A poet once said that joy and sorrow can have the same shape in the world, my Yusuf," she despairingly broke open the rosebud's petals with her delicate fingertips, "for the rose can be an open heart or a broken heart."

"What are the meaning of these words, my Jamila," he came at her with care, "and this sadness?"

"When the rose vanishes from the garden in autumn it is easy to find again in the oil of rosewater, which reminds the heart of a friend."

"Is there a friend missing from your heart?" Yusuf asked warily.

Jamila lifted up her solemn eyes to him.

"Yes, my Yusuf, more than a friend. It is you."

Yusuf weakly shook his head with a blank stare.

"What has pained you and why do I see you so changed?"

"My heart aches and I am not well."

"What weighs on your mind so to make your heart unwell?"

"You know that a woman—if she has a desire for a thing—no one can overcome her," she calmly affirmed. "Nor can anyone set a guard over her, or shelter her, or bar her from the bath or anything else, or from doing all that she sets her heart on."

"And is there a thing you have set your heart on, my Jamila?"

"My Yusuf," she stopped staring down at her own wringing hands, clutching tightly at Yusuf's sleeves and looking imploringly into his eyes, "I do not know what has happened to me. Nor do I know what you have done to me or how. All I know is that I want to spend my whole life with you and that I wish we could be together always."

"Then confide your cause to Him," Yusuf heartened her, "the Lord who made mankind. Quit your heartache and care and be content of mind, for my wish is the very same. Ask not the past or how or why it came to pass. All human things are by fate and destiny designed!"

"Only I fear my fate and destiny lie very far away from you, my Yusuf," she lamented, heaving a sorrowful sigh. "And there is no help for it, for my father is giving me away in marriage and I am betrothed to another."

Yusuf looked abruptly and deeply heart-stricken.

"But can you not overcome this burden as you yourself cannot be overcome?"

"My Yusuf," she answered assuredly, "I would marry you

this very day if I could and would never give you up, never let you go. But because of what my marriage means to my father, and what it means to keeping peace between two opposing kingdoms—my own and that of my betrothed—then it is I who am overcome."

"Then my heart aches as painfully as your own. And as the poet has said: when God wills a thing to come to a man who is gifted with reason and hearing and sight, He deafens his ears, and blinds his sight, and draws his reason from him like a hair, until having fulfilled His purpose against him, He restores his reason that he may be warned."

"And when the tyranny of fate will most oppress you take heart, for one day will gladden you, one madden you."

"Then what will we do, my darling?" Yusuf's voice sounded full of despair.

"Let us cherish the moment," Jamila hung down her head forlornly, "and this night together, for I could die tomorrow."

"Do not dare speak of your death, my beloved, or surely I will die."

"But why can I not have the one I love?" Jamila cried. "Why can I not be with the one I love? I hate myself for being who I am! So much I wish I could die! And I would rather die than live without you!"

"But you know you cannot die," Yusuf said in a defeated tone, "for if you die too much of the world will die with you and all will be lost. At least this way only our hearts will be lost."

"To me the loss of your heart is all the world I have," Jamila's grieving eyes welled out with tears. "Come. Let me show you the place where my heart wants to stay when it dies."

§

A conical-shaped and smooth-faced peak, the steepest pinnacle on the Isle of Pearl soared to a towering and tapering point which abruptly shot up and punctured the heavens. Close to its lofty summit narrow stone steps carved out of roughhewn rock rose tortuously high up the sheer cliff in a rugged and serpentine footpath, leading directly to a small, black gaping hole in the seaward side. Beyond the breach from deep inside the gouged hollow of rock Jamila and Yusuf could look out and watch the brightened canopy of heaven throw its illuminating light upon the shimmering sea spreading boundlessly below.

Together they lay close, clothed and covered by a silk sheet upon a satin mattress stuffed with raw silk, pensively listening and brooding upon the soft sigh of the sea and the wheezing wail of the wind outside. From inside their dark, snug and quiet cavity they could distinctly see the all-encompassing celestial spaces light up and overspread the nocturnal earth. Once more they sank deeper into their ostrich-down pillows and velvet-embroidered cushions as they warmly embraced. When their lips softly touched—their faces mildly aglow from the dim and mellow light of flickering candles—they lingered to taste and savor the melting warmth of their deeply impassioned breaths.

"I love your kisses," Jamila sighed.

"I love to kiss you," Yusuf softly ran a finger across her fervid, quivering lips. "We have been lying here for hours and I have hardly felt time pass."

"We must love each other very much."

"Yes."

"Do you still love me even though we cannot make love?" she looked up at him with deeply exploring eyes.

"As profoundly as I love the Lord God who gave us our love," he solemnly professed, "the First Cause and Creator of all things!"

"I have thought about you being here with me often," she confided. "And now I wish to keep you with me, for I have never loved anyone like this before."

"Nor I," he tenderly caressed her cheek.

"Then let us be married, for in my heart I am already your wife."

"No, my Jamila," he shook his head hopelessly. "You cannot be my wife. You can never be my wife."

"I am," she insisted. "I am more."

"Since when have you become my wife, my dear Jamila?"

"Since we first met," she answered surprisingly. "Come. Let me show you a thing."

Languidly Jamila arose and held up a lighted wax taper to dimly illuminate an inscription engraved upon the unpolished cave wall:

> *Dear is the wet diver to the eyes of his pale wife,*
> *Who waits and weeps on shore by*
> *the sand of the wine-dark sea.*
> *Plunging all day in the deep blue waves.*
> *And at night, having gathered up his toll of precious pearls.*
> *Rejoins her in their cave on the shore.*

"My dear Yusuf," she said seriously, "I want so much for you to rejoin and remain with me here in this cave on the shore as my husband."

"You should have a care about what you say," Yusuf cautioned her, "for a marriage needs no witness to be lawful."

"My beloved," she persisted, "you have wounded my heart and love of you has taken possession of it. And from the time I first saw you neither sleep nor food nor drink has been pleasant to me."

"And more than that do I feel, for the state in which I am needs no complaint to bear witness to it."

Kneeling upon the mattress before him Jamila tightly grasped Yusuf's right hand with her own, nudged his thumb to rise to touch hers and firmly pressed both their thumbs together.

"Great would be my happiness if we pledged our marriage-vow to each other with no one for our witness but God," she betrothed herself in earnest, "for even though we cannot be together I love you very, very much!"

Yusuf gazed upon her just as earnestly.

"Then I ask."

"And I give," she exclaimed, "By God and by the life of His Prophet I give myself to you!"

"And I take," Yusuf showed a warm smile.

"And I take you," she consented heartily, "as witness against me with God also my witness that I will never desert you. And you will see the truth of my words even though our marriage must be a secret. So keep this our secret."

"No one keeps a secret but one of the faithful," he affirmed. "And even among the best of mankind it remains hidden."

"Our secret is with me as in a house with a lock," she assured him, "whose key is lost and whose door is sealed."

They embraced and kissed deeply.

"I love you! I love you! I love you!" Jamila gasped, breathless. "I swear to God—to almighty Allah—I love you! And I wish I could stay with you all my life!"

Unexpectedly a blinding glow of light flashed at the far off horizon and shot out radiant beams all across the great, glimmering sea. Day broke and a blazing orange sun rose slowly in a great fiery ball at the distant sea line. Their smoldering embrace grudgingly broke with the dawning light of day.

"The sun salutes the Ornament of the Good!" Yusuf praised. "Mohammed the Prophet of God!"

"I will see no good this day," Jamila mourned, "for now I must leave you and go my way."

Sadly, softly, Yusuf stroked tears from Jamila's feverishly warm cheeks.

"Precious is the tear that rains from the sky," he recited ruefully, "which turns into a pearl as it falls into the sea."

"It has been said, my most handsome Yusuf," she deplored, her arms clinging tightly about his neck, "that the teardrops of angels that fall onto the sea and turn into pearls take their color from the heavens—cloudy or clear by the serenity or the gloom of the dawn."

"But this day," she shook her head with grievous sorrow, her languid eyes languishing under the daunting heaviness afflicting her deeply sinking heart, "I will see nothing but the deepest and darkest gloom."

EPILOGUE:
CHARIOT OF THE SUN

WOMEN

"Allah commands you to hand back your trusts to their rightful owners, and to pass judgment upon men with fairness. Noble is that to which Allah exhorts you. He hears all and observes all."—Surah IV, 58

"A friendly and free and ample welcome to you, my venerable vizier!" King Freton greeted Bahram—his guest from the Land of the Red King—in his crystal cave audience hall. "Rejoice at the performing of your affair and let your heart be contented and delighted, and your eyes be joyful and happy, and your breast be gladdened and swollen!"

"May your power and glory endure for ages and evermore," Bahram saluted the king of the Isle of Pearl, reverently kissing his fingertips and raising them to his brow. "I have come for the fulfillment of my king's demand."

"You fail in respect to me by making your demand," King Freton, outwardly offended by the visiting vizier's brashness, berated him, "and it is plain that your understanding is of the meanest and most mercenary, and that you are in want of good manners. I would never give away my daughter in marriage for even her weight in gold—not even to keep from my lips the cup of death. But God does whatever He wills."

"My king," Bahram objected politely, "do not imagine that I brought you this demand fearing anything or craving anything, for the truth is that I concluded that the Princess Jamila was not suitable to anyone but my king."

"Even so," the king subtly persisted once more, "tell me again: have you seen in your time such overwhelmingly perfect and pure pearls as the ones I offered you?"

"Never saw I such, my lord," Bahram readily admitted. "Nor do I believe that there are in the treasures of our lord—the Red King of the Land—a single one like them."

"Ah!" the king sighed with emphatic disgust. "Enough for me this situation I am in! Why do you not take pity on me and spare my beloved daughter this demand!"

"When my king first cast his eyes on her portrait he lost himself on her as he desired but all too well," Bahram recounted after a crisp pause for reflection, "for since the time he looked on her, my king of the age, to this very hour life has not been pleas-

209

ant to him. And he has demanded of me that I ask her to wife for him, because his coveting of her has mastered his vitals and to such a degree that he said to me, 'Know you, Grand Vizier of mine, that if I do not win my wish, surely I will die.'"

King Freton sat silent and sullen; the Grand Vizier looked equally solemn and grim-faced.

"You can no longer buy off the buyer by paying the buyer a high price and higher," Bahram said in deadly earnest.

"Then she is his handmaiden," the king conceded grudgingly, his face expressing severe vexation and soreness. "I give her away in marriage to him to take to wife and he will do me honor by taking her. And I beg to God—whose name be exalted!—that I may have the joy of marrying my daughter to your king. So what do you say?"

"The thing should be as you judge," the Grand Vizier answered staidly. "By their union—and their children—your memory will be preserved."

"My honorable vizier and dignified lord," the king wheezed heavily with a long-suffering sigh, "hear now what I have to say. We are to the Red King of the Land among the number of his lieges and we will be ennobled by his alliance and affiliation. We crave this distinction and my daughter is one of his handmaidens. This is our greatest wish and noblest need that he may be our reliance."

Nodding the king demandingly beckoned to his own vizier—Faris—to step up and attend to them.

"There is no help but that we recite the Fatihah and perform the contract of marriage," King Freton announced gravely. "My own honorable vizier will act as my daughter's deputy and a devout witness will write and seal the contract."

"So be it," Bahram nodded his accord.

Faris moved toward Bahram, gestured to the floor and together the two sat down upon the carpet facing each other. He grasped Bahram's right hand with his own, raising their thumbs and pressing them together. An aged, grayheaded *Kadee*—a minister of marriage—came up and overlaid their joined hands with an oblong handkerchief—each of its twin edges embroidered with a fringe of colored silk and gold.

Resistantly, repugnantly, reluctantly—the king's lips quivered to give utterance to the dreaded and forbidding words.

"I betroth to you my daughter, Jamila," he muttered, "the virgin Princess of the Sea, for the dowry you have so generously and graciously given."

Looking perversely pleased and satisfied Bahram lifted up his expressive eyes to the king.

"I accept from you her betrothal to my king."

So stricken in years the aged Kadee sluggishly lifted up his hands in praise of Allah and dictated to the rest the prayer they would recite together:

> *In the Name of Allah, The Compassionate, The Merciful!*
> *Praise be to Allah, Lord of the Creation*
> *The Compassionate, The Merciful,*
> *King of Judgment-day!*
> *You alone we worship, and to You alone we pray for help.*
> *Guide us to the straight path,*
> *The path of those Whom You have favored,*
> *Not of those who have incurred Your wrath,*
> *Nor of those who have gone astray.*

Just as suddenly and uncontrollably the king's weary and saddened eyes burst out with painfully soft, silent tears.

§

From the twin-towered gatehouse perched precipitously high atop the sheer stony shelf, overlooking the great and bounding sea tossing about wildly far off below, the heavy timber drawbridge clanged down and spanned the cavernous chasm plummeting deep between the sea cliff and the cragged column towering by it—solidly shoring up a level table of roughhewn rock. Chains clanked along turning pulleys as the weighty timber-and-iron trelliswork portcullis-grating was raised, budging and grinding gradually upwards. Out of the arched gateway burst four gleaming and powerfully built white Arabian horses, their colorful fly-whisk head-plumes bending backwards in the wind, briskly drawing a blazing bronze chariot.

Bahram demandingly drove the team. He yanked back on the bridle reins and the spirited steeds, their eyes flashing brightly and their arched necks and heads held high, champed at their jointed snaffle-bits and pranced proudly to a fitful stop. Bahram climbed down from the D-shaped platform of the chariot box, leaving the reins overhanging the vertical bar dividing the chariot's front curved panel into two equal halves. He checked the yoke fastenings and handled the pairs of ringed tassels hanging in globules from the team's necks. Then he turned to graciously greet the short procession of people passing ceremoniously through the castle gateway.

King Freton drew near in company with his daughter, Jamila, wholly veiled in a cashmere shawl, his vizier, Faris, their palace guards and attendants.

"As a charioteer," the king pronounced, stepping up directly to Bahram, "you have been our most honored and respected guest. The three-day term of hospitality is at an end. And after two days of rest your day of departure has come."

"It is well," Bahram affirmed, motioning exultantly to the glinting chariot. "And my chariot is desirous of glory. Behold— the Celestial Chariot of the Sun!"

"Most praiseworthy is your chariot's greatness and grandeur," the king complimented him, "for surely your chariot is a sign of your kingdom's imperial strength."

"The chariot of the gods is ageless, immortal and world-conquering!" Bahram boasted. "It is deserving of veneration and praise. The great god Mithra rides upon its wheels. It will make the journey to the final place of no return; the final crossing of the gods; the far end of the road. And its destination is the world of heaven."

"How will you go?" King Freton looked careworn.

"We will take flight and follow the river of the sky eastward, for eastward is the path that leads to the gods and the world of heaven. And we will follow this course."

"But like the man who walks with only one foot does not the chariot that flies without wings come to harm?"

"The carpenter of the chariot is rather like the composer of songs of praise. Just as songs of praise are well-composed a celestial chariot is well-carpentered. And this chariot is yoked for a wheeled journey to the world of heaven where we will come to safety in the dwelling place of the gods."

"But is not such a river-crossing a perilous affair, for when you leave our realm you will be left by the gods and perhaps be confronted with demons of the sky?"

"We will fly swiftly with the speed of the falcon as doves fly bound for water-springs!" Bahram simpered. "And we will be impossible to overtake, for a chariot fitted with the fastenings of the gods will reach its desired destination."

He stepped to the side of the chariot and gestured casually to its great spoked wheels.

"Just as heaven and earth are pushed apart the axle pushes apart the wheels of the chariot. So the earth, the wind and the heavens must be yoked and bound firmly together. And just as the chariot-wheel creaks if not steadied the worlds above and below can be unfirm and unsteadied."

He laid hold of one of the thick and heavy spokes and heaved hard against it. Spiritedly the horses started, budging the chariot box forward.

"But the wheels of this chariot are steady. And an auspicious axle is one that is oiled, firm and does not creak."

He stepped to the front of the horses and laid hold of one of their headstalls, wrenching it tight. Friskily the horses snorted and bobbed their heads.

"And so too must the yoke and thongs be fast and secure as they are."

King Freton stepped up to the horses, marveling at them with admiring eyes.

"Tradition tells us that God gave Suleyman one hundred winged horses from the sea which are said to be specially blessed with good fortune, but like true friends fine steeds are few—even if to the eye of the inexperienced they are many."

"Have no fear," Bahram heartened him. "These striding sun-finder horses will pull the sun-finding chariot and win the prize of the sun!"

"Set out on your journey, my vizier, in prosperity and good fortune, and health and safety," the king bade him fair, turning to cast his somber eyes on his grim-faced daughter. "I commend you to Him with whom deposits are not lost."

"He who has knowledge and thought which is pure will reach that abode from which there is no rebirth—the far end of the road; the final place," Bahram invoked. "And drawn by these horses this chariot will carry the nuptial fire on its journey to its new home, for the tainted must take away the tainted to become glorious!"

King Freton drew near Jamila, gently taking her face into his hands and softly kissing her between her eyes, spilling with tears.

"What state is this I see you in?"

"Here with you I live in the Heaven of heavens," Jamila mourned, "but taking my leave of you is of hells my Hell."

"Such is the world, so bear a patient heart when riches leave and when dear ones depart!" the king exhorted her.

Jamila hung down and shook her head spiritlessly.

"Words cannot undo the done," the king consoled her, "for the reed of Destiny has run through what God has decreed. Just know, my daughter, there is nothing dearer to me than you."

Linked to the golden chariot box was an ornate, four-wheeled cart covered by an arched canopy and gilded just beneath its rail with a decorative, zigzagging band. Her face streaming with tears Jamila resigned herself to her handmaidens who helped her mount the cart and seat herself upon a mattress-covered divan. Blankly she stared down.

"Because we will fly on the cloud of Fate," Bahram informed the king, stepping up to him, "the Land of the Red King will be but a day's journey away."

"Hear me then," the king bluntly confronted the vizier, "there is a newcomer among us who has suffered misadventures at sea, because of which I have a mind to speed his return to his native land, which borders on the Land of the Red King, so he will ever bless me and pray for me."

"Who is this newcomer?" Bahram looked richly surprised.

"He is one of the janizary—our palace guard. He will accompany you and be as your escort until he can return to his fatherland."

"And where is this young man who is minded to journey with us to our kingdom?" Then he looked richly affronted.

"He is your servant and he stands before you!" His answer came from an unfamiliar voice.

Momentarily speechless Bahram wheeled about to curiously watch the young guard step away from the train of attendants and come up to the chariot. He wore a short coat of mail—a jacket covered with satin but heavily padded and studded with rectangular, overlapping splint armor—reaching just to his waist. Two pieces of steel with iron fingers, fitting into each other, covered his arms from his elbows downwards. An iron helmet covered his head. He carried a round and bossed metal shield. From a shoulder belt he carried his straight double-edged long-sword—damascened with silver steel. It was Yusuf!

"Make haste," Bahram snapped with a reconciled but disconcerted tone, "for the wind is fair!"

"I hear and obey."

"It is as you wish," Bahram grudgingly assured the king.

"My Yusuf!" a man called out to him.

Yusuf turned about to meet Malik, master pearl diver, dressed like him in the janizary sword and uniform.

"If you truly have a mind to journey to your native land," he accosted him, smiling, "no one will hinder you, so do as you will."

"I cannot do better than journey with these travelers," Yusuf shrugged stoically.

"You are your own master," Malik affirmed, "but if ever it is your will to live here among us—on our head and eyes be it—for you gladden our hearts with your fellowship. Ask then what you will and I will grant you the very same."

"By God, my lord, you have truly overwhelmed me with your favors and good will. But I long for a sight of my native country. And I have nothing to ask of you but your remembrance."

"And I you. You cheer us with your company, my son, but praised be God for your safety and safe conduct!"

Affectionately Malik touched Yusuf's head as he bowed to kiss his master's hand and sleeve.

"My God, my uncle," Yusuf choked, "you have become to me even as my own father."

Without looking back Yusuf left Malik to mount the chariot together with Faris, the king's grand vizier, and Malik looked after them, making a wry face. Before mounting the chariot cart Yusuf paused to inspect the bloated, bronzed bull's heads protruding ominously from the chariot's bridle bosses and yoke saddles. Finally Bahram mounted the chariot box and pulled the reins, spurring his spirited steeds with the bridle spit's ivory points.

"Up with you and obey the rein!" he barked, smartly snapping the reins.

Spry and springy the horses pranced—their effortless gait turning from a floating trot to a smooth canter and then to a mightily free and feathery gallop, bounding over the tableland with ground-leaping strides. Finally the spirited steeds and chariot sprang together with one leap into the breezy air and scaled the dizzying heights of the bright blue sky.

Out upon her lofty, windswept terrace Fatima the devotee sauntered to the balustrade overlooking the vast blue sea, carrying her majestic white falcon upon her gauntleted wrist. Intently she watched the golden chariot vault into the heavens and retreat from sight.

"In the name of God—God is the Mightiest!" she cried, loosening the falcon's silken, gold-embroidered jesses and hood, jingling their tiny silver bells. Jauntily she pointed to the flying chariot. "Ouye, ouye, ouye! There it is!"

At one jump the feisty falcon soared sky-high and with ear-splitting outcries swooped down upon the chariot, plummeting past it in a daunting nosedive.

"Godspeed, my Yusuf," Fatima thought out aloud, watching the chariot readily ascend the heavens, "you who seeks severance. Draw the rein of your swift steed, for treachery is the rule of life. And the sweets of meeting end in severance."

From beneath the chariot canopy Yusuf looked out over the rail at Fatima's swift-flying falcon as the bird shot past them and across the craggy cliffs and tossing seas so far off below. He glanced only fleetingly at Jamila, sitting quietly across from him together with Faris, her grand vizier. Blustering wind streamed across their solemn faces.

"Self-esteem is his only counselor," Yusuf muttered to himself, understanding by a certain proverb the meaning of Fatima's departing farewell, "the only motive for his actions. He is not hungry and instead of hunting will regain his freedom."

Tears flowed from even Fatima's saddened eyes as she fared Yusuf well one last time.

"Remember to pray for God's saving intercession, my Yusuf," she murmured as if he could hear her. "Remember to raise your voice and say the *Celestial Verses!*"

To Be Continued...Jamila and Yusuf will return
in ***Arabian Nights Lost: Celestial Verses II***

.

www.ingramcontent.com/pod-product-compliance
Lightning Source LLC
Chambersburg PA
CBHW030519020726
47494CB00004B/1160